W9-ACJ-868

By the same author

The Island of Animals

Fate of a Prisoner

AND OTHER STORIES

DENYS JOHNSON-DAVIES

Quartet Books

First published by Quartet Books Limited in 1999
A member of the Namara Group
27 Goodge Street
London W1P 2LD

ISBN 0 7043 8118 4

Phototypeset by FSH Ltd
Printed and bound in Great Britain by Cox & Wyman, Reading Berks

Contents

Fate of a Prisoner

AND OTHER STORIES

1
The Dream

James Murphy paid off the taxi alongside the British Embassy, then crossed the traffic coming down from the Corniche and walked down the four steps into the grocery. Having bought a bottle of dark-green olive oil marked Extra Virgin, and a packet a chocolate biscuits manufactured in Holland on the grocer's personal recommendation, he retraced his steps past the embassy and made a precarious passage through the several lanes of traffic that were on their way past the capital's main luxury hotels.

The heat of summer had just begun. That morning he had decided that the time had come to wear his dark glasses and Panama hat. He was self-conscious, feeling that they made him look like a

1

tourist – he who had been living in Cairo for nearly half a century.

He made his way into the labyrinth of streets that was Garden City. The Nubian doorman stood up as he entered the iron gateway and passed through a dusty garden to the front entrance. As he got into the cool and began the climb of two flights of stairs, he wiped away the sweat from his forehead. He arrived at his front door breathless and slightly dizzy. Instead of searching for his keys he rang the bell and the door was opened almost immediately by the cook, Abdul Ghaffar, who also doubled as houseboy.

'Too hot, doktor,' Abdul Ghaffar commented, giving his master the honorary doctorate accorded in Egypt to most of those connected with the teaching profession. His master grunted his agreement, handed over his purchases and went immediately to the bathroom. He ran the cold tap and splashed his face and sparse white hair. In the bedroom he removed his dusty shoes, put on his slippers and settled down in the living-room with the *Egyptian Gazette* and the two letters that had been delivered that morning to the school and which he had kept unread till now.

Abdul Ghaffar's gaunt form appeared in the glass doorway that opened into the dining area. He placed on the table a tray with a bottle of Stella beer, its neck glistening with cold beads, a tall glass and a bowl of roasted peanuts.

'Make *hisab* now, doktor?' Abdul Ghaffar asked.

The two of them, master and servant, conversed in a language that had evolved over the years, a mixture of pidgin English and the occasional mispronounced Arabic word. It was of course ridiculous, he told himself, that a man of education, a man who had spent the greater part of his life in Egypt, a man who had, no less, a financial interest in a language school, could not make himself understood in the language of the country. His excuse – one he often gave when the topic of learning foreign languages came up in conversation – was that you either made a serious effort at learning the language properly – reading, writing, the lot – or you left it well alone.

'*Baadein*, Abdul Ghaffar,' he answered, indicating that he would do the accounts later. He made no attempt at pronouncing the guttural 'gh' in his servant's name, this being part of his 'leaving it well alone'.

'OK, doktor,' said Abdul Ghaffar and retired to the kitchen.

Carefully pouring out the beer, James Murphy told himself, as he did each lunch-time, that however pleasant a bottle of Stella was, especially in summer, it invariably meant that he spent an hour or so in the afternoon asleep and would wake with the sort of mouth he knew from the days when he had been a smoker. The drinking of alcohol should be restricted, as Britain's colonizing forebears had discovered, to the hours after the going down of the sun.

He looked at the top of the front page of the newspaper and confirmed that it was Thursday, the day on which, twice a month, his Coptic friend Nabil came to drinks, dinner and several games of chess. While he and Abdul Ghaffar had not agreed what dinner should consist of, he felt sure that his cook had not, like himself, forgotten about it.

'Abdul Ghaffar!' he called and almost immediately the man was conjured up before him, drying his hands on a dishcloth. Sometimes he wondered whether Abdul Ghaffar was able to read his mind. 'Mr Nabil come dinner,' James Murphy informed him and Abdul Ghaffar acknowledged the fact with an inclination of his head. 'What you cook, Abdul Ghaffar?'

'Fish in oven,' Abdul Ghaffar informed him. 'Bolti, very good, very new fish.' Bolti, James Murphy had learnt, was a Nile fish that Abdul Ghaffar prepared very tastily in the oven with sliced potatoes, onions and tomatoes. He also knew that 'new' meant 'fresh'.

'And for sweet, Abdul Ghaffar?' Abdul Ghaffar's repertoire of desserts was limited. 'Caramel custard?' he ventured.

'Caramelly custar,' acknowledged Abdul Ghaffar.

'And for starters?'

'Cocktail shrimp?'

'*Kwais, kwais,*' pronounced James Murphy. It was

an unwritten law that suggested menus were not open to discussion.

James Murphy turned to his post. He was just unfolding the first of the two letters, both of which bore Irish stamps, when the thought came to him that he should put a bottle of white wine in the fridge – the sooner the better because Egyptian white wine was drinkable only when any possible taste it might have had was nullified by extreme cooling. He put the letter aside, took a bottle of Cleopatra from the cupboard and placed it alongside the row of Stella beers on the bottom shelf. Though he did not care for Egyptian wine, his Coptic guest seemed to like it and foreign wine was either unobtainable or impossibly expensive; alas, he no longer had a close contact in the embassy who could supply him with the occasional duty-free bottle.

He passed by the kitchen to tell Abdul Ghaffar that he had put a bottle of wine in the fridge and that it should be opened only when the first course was served. He found his cook standing by the kitchen table wearing a pair of his master's discarded sunglasses with broken frames for the operation of chopping up the onions. Abdul Ghaffar removed them momentarily when addressed.

The handwriting on both envelopes was immediately recognizible. On one was the uneven scrawling hand of his neighbour in the Kerry village where he had his cottage. Michael Moriarty, who lived with his twin brother and younger sister in an identical cottage to his own farther up the lane, had from the beginning assumed charge of his house and had each year protested with genuine vehemence against accepting a gift of money for his services. Michael's task of caretaking included lighting turf fires upstairs and downstairs if the weather turned really cold (which it invariably did), letting the electricity man in to read the meter, and putting down rat poison. He also wrote two or three letters a year to the 'Dublin man from Cairo, Egypt', as, only half in jest, he referred to him, reporting on the state of the cottage, the state of the weather and any local gossip he thought might be of interest. The present letter stated that the weather had seldom been worse but that the cottage had stood up well except for the loss of a few tiles, which he had replaced; that it didn't look as if they'd have much of a harvest this year but that, please God, it would hold for a spell in the summer to allow them to get the hay in. Paddy hadn't been too well with his back and had had to go to Tralee for treatment, but Mrs Sullivan farther up the valley with the b. & b. was on the mend, thanks be to God, and was being helped by her niece who had come down from Ennis to join her. He had taken up the boat and would give it a lick of paint directly he had the time and the weather looked set for a couple of fine days. Would he be wanting the inside done in that same grey colour, that's if they still had any more of it at the garage shop? The fishing had been very poor, very poor indeed. He couldn't remember when it had been so poor. They all looked forward to seeing him soon in good health, please God; he had had the man in to overhaul the pump and had put some lime in the well.

Michael's letters warmed his heart: they reminded him that across the seas, in a country more unlike Egypt than anywhere he could imagine, lay the only piece of property he owned, a cottage he had bought in a state of dilapidation and rescued from encroaching nettles, brambles and ivy. Luckily for him, the locals had acquired a taste for living in newly constructed bungalows and he had been able to secure the cottage and a one-acre field for a few hundred pounds. Michael's letters reminded him that in that bleakly spectacular part of the Ring of Kerry he had friends who had accepted him as one of themselves; the fact that he was originally from Dublin did not of itself give him any such right; being from Dublin made him into as much of a foreigner as the Germans and Dutch who had built themselves barrack-like houses in the area.

The other letter was from his sister in Cork. Younger than him, she had been a widow for many years and had recently moved from Dublin to be near her daughter and grandchildren. Each summer he would stay several days with her before completing his journey to Kerry. Her letter was in reply to his last one in which he had mentioned, for the first time, that he was in two minds about continuing to live in Cairo, that maybe the time had come for him to settle in Ireland. While acknowledging that he was of course fond of Cairo after all these years, she was insistent that a man could have only one home and that his was obviously his Kerry cottage; it wasn't enough, she assured him, that he had spent most of his life in Egypt. Her remark reminded him that in Cairo he would always remain a tourist. After all, he was Irish and it was only reasonable for him to retire to his Irish roots. If he made his home in Kerry, there was nothing to stop him, in the worst of the weather when he felt deprived of sun, taking a trip to somewhere like Spain. All sorts of people these days were taking their holidays in places like Spain and Cyprus.

The two letters filled him with nostalgia for the softness of the speech of the Kerryman and the grandeur of the landscape. How could he be but a stranger in a country where the people talked in raised, seemingly quarrelsome voices and in a language he did not understand? And Cairo? How had he developed this affection for a city all of whose splendours lay in the past and which was today notable only for its pollution and creaking infrastructure?

Cairo had become his home by a fortuitous circumstance. The Suez Crisis, which had upset the lives of so many people, had left his own virtually untouched but had determined its future course. Having graduated from Trinity College, Dublin, and done a couple of years' teaching at a preparatory school in Kent, he had gone to Egypt at the age of twenty-four and had signed up with the Egyptian government to teach for two years. These he had spent uncomfortably at a secondary school in Assiout. He had then agreed to serve a further two years provided he was transferred to a school in Cairo. This had no sooner happened than the political crisis had disrupted the lives and threatened the livelihood of many of the foreigners in Egypt. The English teachers, many of whom had come to regard Egypt as their home, were given one-way tickets to the UK. James Murphy had expected the same treatment and it had needed the Egyptian authorities to remind him that he was Irish and that Egypt, sharing with Ireland a hatred of the British oppressor, was only too happy for him to stay on. Furthermore, because numerous vacancies had suddenly been created, the Egyptian government was prepared to offer him a post at the university. Though the pay differed little from what he had been receiving as a secondary-school teacher, the number of hours he was expected to put in was considerably smaller. At this stage he began to see Cairo and his lectureship at the university in a more permanent light. He had decided to acquire, for a minuscule sum, the right to live at a controlled rent in a flat in Garden City, a district whose area of garden had diminished with the years but which lay conveniently in the centre of the rapidly expanding capital. It was during this time that he had taken on Abdul Ghaffar, a Nubian servant who had previously been passed from one British Embassy official to another as tours of duty ended.

The fifties and sixties had been difficult years. Nasser had imposed an austere lifestyle on his pleasure-loving subjects and a ban on the importation of so-called luxuries, which included items that most Europeans would regard as necessities. Life for those few foreigners who remained in Cairo, without the restaurants and bars run by Greeks, Cypriots and Italians, became drab. Suddenly James Murphy's services as a teacher of English were much in demand. One of his best-paying pupils was a major, closely connected with the coup, who provided him with the necessary sense of security through these erratic times, augmented by an occasional present from the outside world, generally in the form of a bottle of Scotch.

Not being an Egyptian national, James Murphy enjoyed the privilege of being able to travel abroad every year and of taking with him sufficient funds to see him through the months of his summer vacation. It was on one such vacation that he had bought the cottage in Kerry.

Once Sadat came to power and Egypt was again opened up to foreign influence and the vagaries of capitalism, life became easier if more expensive. Little changed in his own life except that he became aware that Abdul Ghaffar was now able to provide him with greater variety in his meals. It was during the early years of Sadat that he had been persuaded by an Egyptian friend to risk some of his capital in setting up with him one of the first of a number of schools devoted to the teaching of English. The school had achieved immediate success and in its second year he had resigned from the university in order to give it his full attention. Suddenly, to his surprise, he had found himself earning more than he required for his daily needs. He had not enjoyed the experience as much as he had imagined: somehow, it seemed to take the edge off life. He could think of nothing to spend the extra money on beyond buying himself a more powerful outboard motor and a new fibreglass fly-rod and adding a garage/storeroom to the cottage. He had also increased Abdul Ghaffar's wages and had given him a lump sum with which to buy himself some land in the village near Aswan from where he came and where his daughter and her husband had settled.

James Murphy was past forty when love and marriage had unexpectedly entered his life. He had by then come to terms with the prospect of spending his life alone. After all, back in Ireland, he had told himself, many a man remained on his own to work a small farm that had to be passed on to other members of the family, while many a girl gave up her years of youth to looking after an aged parent. In Cairo he had formed relationships with two or three women, but there had not been sufficient enthusiasm on one side or the other for it to develop into marriage. Egypt, after all, was not a country in which most women would have ambitions of setting up house, and unmarried foreign women were in short supply. However, an Englishwoman from Cornwall, a teacher at a secondary school for girls and three years his senior, had suddenly entered his life and fulfilled all his requirements in a wife: she was good company, he enjoyed sharing a double bed with her, she made an effort at learning how to fly-fish and did not feel sick or frightened if a storm blew up on the lake; also, she did not try to boss Abdul Ghaffar. Then, after a mere two years, and with the abruptness with which she had sailed into his life, she had weighed anchor and made her departure – covered over by a sheet in the Anglo-American Hospital. It had seemed futile, an impertinence to her memory, to seek a repetition of something so perfect. Dazed by the loss, he gave away all her personal possessions, made up a small album of photographs, and reverted to his bachelor state.

Abdul Ghaffar, feeling he did not have the right to mourn the death of his master's wife, had shed tears in the privacy of the kitchen, not so much for the woman who had briefly shared their life as for the sadness that now shrouded his master.

Faced with having to make a decision about leaving Egypt, one that he should perhaps have made many years ago, first when his English colleagues had been sent away and later when his wife had died, he was at a loss. His was a life that seemed to contain so few alternatives. Perhaps his sister was right and the time had come, now that he had reached the age of sixty-five, to dispose of his interest in the language school in order to spend his final years in retirement among his own people, in a house that belonged to him and in a village into which he had been accepted.

Having lunched sparsely off cheese and salad followed by water-melon, a paperback thriller propped against the water jug, his mind continued to worry at the decision he had set himself. He returned to the living-room for his cup of Turkish coffee. As he took the final sip and removed some grounds from his tongue, he became aware of Abdul Ghaffar standing in the doorway.

'Of course, time for *hisab*, Abdul Ghaffar,' and he took the red account book and the Biro and began noting down the items as they were dictated to him: cauliflower 3, eggs 8, *shammam* 12 – the list went down the whole of one column, what with milk and meat and fish and the washerwoman and matches and something he took to be washing-up cloths and some sort of liquid that Abdul Ghaffar used for putting down the lavatory. As usual the list was endless, and the arithmetic mind-boggling. Not for the first time, it struck him how futile this weekly routine was, for he had implicit faith in both Abdul Ghaffar's honesty and arithmetic. But this procedure had been observed every Thursday for nearly forty years and he knew that Abdul Ghaffar expected it of him. He made the appearance of adding up all the items, then glanced at Abdul Ghaffar. 'Sixty-four bound, twenty-five biastre,' pronounced Abdul Ghaffar, and they agreed that he still had fifteen pounds and seventy-five piastres left. James Murphy handed over a further sixty pounds.

'Oh, and . . . Abdul Ghaffar . . .'

Abdul Ghaffar had not moved: it was as though he had sensed that there was a further matter to be dealt with.

'Abdul Ghaffar, me old man, you old man . . .'

'Yes, doktor,' agreed Abdul Ghaffar, his face breaking into a smile in obvious delight that he and his master had both succeeded in attaining to ripeness.

'Enough work, Abdul Ghaffar, enough *shughl*. You tired, me tired. Now time for rest.'

James Murphy looked up in the hope of receiving some sort of reaction, a hint as to how he should proceed.

'Rest no good, doktor. Allah make man for *shughl*.'

'No, Abdul Ghaffar, me go back home.'

'For summer, doktor, like every summer. You go Englan, me go village.'

'No, Abdul Ghaffar, this time me go for good.' Realizing that this would not be understood, or would be misunderstood, he added: 'For always. Me leave Egypt.'

Abdul Ghaffar's long, deeply lined face assumed a look of disbelief. 'Alway? How alway?' he enquired. 'Doktor have big school, much student.'

James Murphy shook his head: it was proving more difficult than he had envisaged.

'I'm going back home,' he said firmly, reverting in his helplessness to normal English.

'Here home' – and Abdul Ghaffar pointed ahead of him to the space of stone floor that separated them.

'Me go Ireland.'

'Englan,' Abdul Ghaffar gently corrected him, for James Murphy had never made any attempt to explain the difference between the two countries.

'Me find you other *shughl*, or you go live with your daughter...' He turned to the side table and began putting the letters back into their envelopes.

'Abdul Ghaffar no want other *shughl*, Abdul Ghaffar no want live with daughter' – and as he stood there trying to make known his horror of not being able to continue in his present life, tears welled up in his bloodshot eyes. 'You me go Englan,' he said suddenly in desperation.

James Murphy shook his head slowly from side to side: more a comment to himself than a denial to the other.

'Talk later,' he said and put on his glasses as an indication that the conversation was over. Abdul Ghaffar hesitated a moment, then picked up the tray with the coffee cup and the untouched glass of water. Half an hour later James Murphy heard the back door being closed and knew that his cook had gone to one of the local cafés off Kasr el-Aini where the Nubian servants from the embassies and the hotels congregated.

The knowledge that Abdul Ghaffar would not be back before evening released the trap-door to sleep. He slumped in the armchair, legs stretched out, mouth slightly open. Sometimes, especially when he fell asleep of an afternoon, he would dream. He regretted that he was seldom able to recall his dreams, but today, as he wiped the saliva from the side of his mouth, he caught one like a frail butterfly fluttering against a window-pane and passed it to his wakeful mind.

He was fishing on the lake in Kerry. It was a sunny day, too 'hard' as fishermen would say for any chance of a fish, and he was trolling the flies on one side of the boat and the spinner with a silver Meps on the other, while the outboard motor dawdled at his back, so slowly he was fearful it might stall.

Suddenly the stone placed on the bottom of the boat across the line of the fly-rod leapt into the air, the rod bent into a quivering bow, and there was the heart-catching whirr of line being taken out. It was always tricky if you were on your own with two lines out and you got into a fish with one of them: you had to put the engine into neutral, draw in the other line as fast as possible, praying you didn't get into a second fish, and just hope that the fish you'd hooked was still there by the time you got round to playing it. Having successfully wound in the spinner and taken it up, he looked up and saw Abdul Ghaffar sitting directly opposite him, dressed in his white *gallabia* and red cummerbund, and with one of his white skullcaps on his crinkled greying hair. He saw him take up the fly-rod in his right hand, with the index finger holding the line against it so as to keep up the pressure on the fish and managing as though he had had a lifetime's experience of fly-fishing. Once he had the fish under control, he took it round the end of the boat so that it was downstream and would not snarl him up. He brought it in close, the top of the rod straight up and bent like a shepherd's crook, then he lifted the net in his other hand and, taking his time, adroitly netted it. It was a fine sea-trout, something between three and a half and four pounds, with the sea lice still on it.

The dream ended and he opened his eyes to the sound of the muffled hooting of evening traffic passing along the Corniche. He was dazed and slightly out of breath, as though from the anxiety of watching Abdul Ghaffar play the fish and perhaps lose it. Released, the dream made its escape through the meshes of his mind into oblivion.

Just for a few seconds, he had been able to savour the dream: the sparkle of the lake's surface under rare sunshine, the purl of moving water, the embracing mountains stained by the changing shadows of floating clouds. He smiled at the thought of Abdul Ghaffar having been with him on the lake, and this brought back to him the man's suggestion that he should accompany him home to Ireland. It was of course out of the question. How would he manage with the incessant gales off the Atlantic, the cold of the winters? Who would he talk to? Where was the café for him to sit at during his hours off?

Was his sister perhaps right in saying that the mere fact you had spent most of your life in a particular country did not mean that you had become part of it, that it had ousted the country of your birth? But surely you were allowed a choice? There was no law about having to end up where you started from. It was simply a matter of where you preferred to live, which might well be where you had sunk roots of your own tending. And, let's face it, what would he do with himself in that isolated village on the farthest point of the Ring of Kerry once the fishing season closed in October?

If he felt that he wanted to spend more time in his cottage, why should this necessarily mean turning his back on Egypt? What was there to prevent him going to Kerry twice a year instead of just in the summer? Heaven knows, he had the money for two return fares a year. In addition to spending the summer months there, he could also go back for March and April when it was said there was often a good run of sea-trout. Was there anything immoral about having the best of both worlds?

Once again Abdul Ghaffar's tall form entered. He could feel his presence beside him and heard the sound of the tray with teapot, cup and milk jug being placed on the table. He waited till he was no longer aware of the man's presence in the room, then straightened himself and heard his knees crack. As he poured out his cup of tea it occurred to him that he should inform Abdul Ghaffar of his change of mind.

Entering the kitchen, he found Abdul Ghaffar at his prayers. He was sitting back on his bare heels with his large hands resting on his thighs; suddenly his whole body arched over and his forehead touched the end of the prayer carpet. Brought up in a strict religious tradition, James Murphy felt a twinge of regret at his own inability to practise his faith.

In the living-room he stood sipping at his tea and laying out the chess pieces for when his guest arrived. At the same time he kept an ear open for sounds that would tell him that Abdul Ghaffar was once again about his worldly duties. It was only fair to put him out of his misery and tell him that nothing after all would change the routine of their lives.

2
Fate of a Prisoner

Sheikh Mansour bin Khalid bin Abdul Azeem, Ruler of one of the smaller Gulf states, ran his prayer beads through his fingers as he waited for the coffee. Seated to his right in the small private *majlis* overlooking the sea, his Commandant of Police once again asked after the Ruler's health and in turn assured the Ruler that, thanks be to Allah, his own health was fine. Max Poynter knew exactly the reason for his having been summoned at this late hour, but etiquette demanded that any conversation before the ritual drinking of coffee be restricted to mutual enquiries after health.

'And Your Highness's father?' asked Max, conscious that the silence between them required to be broken.

'Thanks be to Allah, Sheikh Khalid is well,' answered the Ruler, glancing towards the open door and changing into a higher gear with his prayer beads. 'And your son?' he asked.

'Thanks be to Allah, he is in good health,' Max replied, though in fact he had not had a letter from him for a couple of weeks.

Both men were grateful to see the bandoliered guard come though the doorway bearing the *dalla* of coffee in his left hand and two diminutive handless cups in his right. A pantomime that had been enacted between the Ruler and his Commandant of Police countless times was gone through yet again as the Ruler waved the proffered cup towards Max, who in turn indicated to the guard that the Ruler be given precedence. As usual, the Ruler gave way and took the first cup. Both contented themselves with a single cup, having shaken it as an indication that a fill-up was not wanted and had handed it back to the guard. The latter, with a deft flick of the wrist, disposed of the dregs to one side on an expensive Qum carpet, a gift to the Ruler's father by a grateful merchant. ·

Once the guard had left, Sheikh Mansour addressed himself to his Commandant of Police: 'Mr Max, it is about the matter we were discussing earlier today.'

On his first being appointed to the post in the sheikhdom he had found the Ruler, unable to pronounce Poynter, calling him Bunter. Tiring of this, Max had one day suggested that he be called from now on by his 'personal' name of Max. The Ruler had readily agreed, finding this name easier to pronounce; he also derived quiet amusement from the alliteration of the name with 'Mr'.

Max had both respect and affection for old Sheikh Mansour. In fact, at fifty-seven or thereabouts the Ruler was no more than three or four years senior to his Commandant of Police, but it was difficult for Max to think of 'the old man' as other than his senior in both years and experience. While Sheikh Mansour would have been incapable of passing the equivalent of an 'O' level in any subject, he had been blessed by birth and had acquired through a difficult reign of some thirty years, following the ousting of his uxorious but incompetent father, a degree of cunning and depth of understanding of his fellow men as would have done credit to the author of *The Prince*. His present excellent relations with his old father, who lived in grand style in a palace in a nearby village, was evidence of his ability to live in harmony with someone who might well be thought to bear him a grudge. In actual fact, once removed from the endless task of keeping at bay the rival tribes that roamed the desert wastes of the sheikhdom and trying to manage somehow to make ends meet without the benefits of oil, Sheikh Khalid had, since being deposed, found himself able to devote all his dwindling energies to servicing the appetites of his regulation four wives.

As Max had supposed, the reason for his having been summoned to the palace was the Omani policeman who had for the past few days been occupying a room in the old Portuguese fort that served the sheikhdom as a prison. The young man was awaiting trial for murder. The killing had been committed in broad daylight and had been witnessed by a number of people. The outcome of a trial was therefore a foregone conclusion and the sentence inevitably one of death. All that had to be decided by the Ruler was when the trial should take place and the manner of execution.

'Yes, may you live long?' said Max, interrupting the silence between them.

'Since morning I have given some thought as to the best way in which to deal with this stupid young man who is causing us such trouble.' Sheikh Mansour struck out at a particularly obstinate fly with his prayer beads, then called to the guard who was seated on a cane chair by the doorway.

'Kill that fly,' ordered the Ruler, and the guard hurried off to bring a fly-swat.

'Much as we may dislike the idea of having a trial,' continued the Ruler, 'I see no way of preventing it. The brother of the dead man came to see me after you left this morning and he is insistent that the matter should go before the *qadi* immediately...'

The Ruler stopped talking and followed the guard's efforts at disposing of the fly. At last, in exasperation, he ordered him to hand over the fly-swat and annihilated the fly with a single blow. The Ruler handed back the swat to the guard, who quickly withdrew.

'We know very well, Mr Max, what the result of a trial would be.'

'Certainly, Your Highness.' In his conversations with the Ruler Max rang the changes between 'Your Highness' and the traditional 'may you live long'. 'The prisoner will be found guilty?'

'What other verdict can there be?' demanded the Ruler. 'And when the *qadi* asks the family of the dead man in accordance with the sharia law whether they want blood-money or blood, we know only too well what the answer will be.'

'Yes, may you live long,' replied Max with a nod of his head, wondering where this unnecessary circumlocution was leading.

'The murdered man's family,' continued the Ruler, 'are not in need of money.'

'And even if they were,' Max pointed out the obvious, 'the prisoner is in no position to pay blood-money.'

'Quite so,' said the Ruler, 'and thus the only alternative is for the prisoner to pay for his folly with his life.'

'That is right, Your Highness,' agreed Max, though he did not altogether go along with Sheikh Mansour's insistence that the young prisoner had acted foolishly: the murder had in fact been committed under severe provocation and there was also the element of honour – all-important where Arabs were concerned.

'And you, Mr Max, as Commandant of Police, will have to make the arrangements for some sort of execution, this in a place where, during the whole of my lifetime, no such thing – thanks be to Allah – has been known. The whole business will cause us both a lot of trouble and will take our minds off more useful and constructive matters.'

His Highness, Max told himself, was taking an unusually long time to come to the point, and he began to feel apprehensive. Realizing that the Ruler was gazing at him expectantly, he muttered, 'Indeed, may you live long.'

'People, as you know, enjoy such spectacles and they may well demand of me that the execution take place in public.' He knew his Commandant of Police well and was not surprised to see Max shake his head slowly from side to side.

'I know that you would not relish such a thing. For this reason I have given much thought to ways in which we could be saved from arranging such a spectacle.'

'I need not remind Your Highness that the foreign press will greatly enjoy writing about the backwardness of the Arabs in these matters.'

The Ruler looked up sharply. 'I have been aware of that too. The West seems to have more sympathy for its criminals than its victims and would like us to share that view. The Omani has killed another man and deserves to die. That is quite clear. However, it is also obvious that a trial and an execution would be exceedingly embarrassing. From everyone's point of view it would be best were he to die in prison.'

'In prison?' queried the Commandant of Police, having failed to anticipate where the Ruler's thoughts were leading.

'By his own hand,' added the Ruler, irritated at having to be so specific.

'By his own hand?' repeated Max, his unease increasing.

The Ruler gave him a stare of feigned surprise. 'I mean – *apparently* by his own hand. You understand? While he sleeps. Such a death would be best for everyone, even for the prisoner himself, don't you agree?'

'Without a trial, Your Highness?' questioned Max innocently.

'Of course without a trial!' exploded the Ruler, increasingly irked at the evident obtuseness of his Commandant of Police. 'If the prisoner dies in the meantime there will be no necessity for either a trial or an execution. The matter will have been taken out of our hands.'

Without waiting for any further comment the Ruler clapped his hands and the guard with the accoutrements of coffee-serving appeared immediately.

'In his sleep,' said the Ruler, before handing back his cup. He then waited till the guard had left the room before adding, 'The man is not from here and there is no one to question how he meets his death. By noon tomorrow he can be buried and forgotten. Arrange everything among your men.' 'Seeing the troubled look on Max's face, Sheikh Mansour added: 'What you should bear in mind is that here is a man for whom, because he has killed another man, death, in one form or another, is inevitable.'

The Ruler rose to his feet, a tall stately figure with a hooked nose and piercing eyes, a man whose presence commanded obedience. He held out his hand and his thin lips broke into a smile as he bid his Commandant of Police good-night.

Zeyd the Omani, a recent recruit to the sheikhdom's police, had ended his brief career by shooting a fellow policeman, one of the four sergeants in the force. Zeyd had been spending much of his time and the greater part of his monthly wages on patronising the services of a young girl who, having mothered a child out of wedlock, had fled from some village in Yemen and taken up prostitution as the sole form of livelihood open to her. Becoming increasingly infatuated with her, Zeyd had seen that the only way in which he could have her for himself was by marrying her. The two had lived for several months happily enough, without the girl being tempted back to her former employment. It seemed, though, that a certain Sergeant Bekheit, a local man who had at one time been a buyer of her favours, had begun to taunt the young husband about his erstwhile relationship with the girl. The day came when the young policeman, on duty in the souk, had been subjected to a ribald remark by the sergeant. In answer he had shot the sergeant twice in the chest and had then run to police headquarters where he had given himself up. Right from the beginning it was obvious to Max that the incident was likely to develop into one of the more unpleasant with which his career as a policeman – firstly in Palestine, then in Bahrain and now with Sheikh Mansour – had been studded. It was being made the more painful for him by the liking he had formed for the young man whom, with superior intelligence and better education than most recruits, he had already singled out for promotion. And now, during the man's days in prison, Max had come to know him better through his daily visits. Though accustomed to the fatalism of many Arabs, the coolness with which Zeyd seemed to face his bleak future aroused his admiration and sympathy. During his first visit, when he had asked Zeyd whether he had any requests, the prisoner had asked for a copy of the Qur'an. He explained that he did of course have one at his home but that he preferred for Max to buy him another one, obviously anxious that no contact be made with his wife. When Max had bought him one in the souk and the prisoner had attempted to pay him, Max had insisted on making him a present of it. The only other request Zeyd had made of him was that he bring him any letters that might come to him addressed to police headquarters, indicating that he was expecting one from his father. When Max had asked him whether he had written home to tell them of what had happened, Zeyd had admitted, with a wry smile and a shake of the head, that he had so far been unable to bring himself to do so.

It became clear to Max that his daily visits, the times of which he varied, were valued by the prisoner. Instructions had been given that Zeyd was to receive no visitors and was not to mix with the other prisoners. His periods for exercise were therefore limited to the times when the rest of the fort's inmates were taken to work in the date gardens of the Ruler's father The following day Max had brought with him a letter bearing an Omani stamp. Zeyd's dark, cleanshaven face had brightened and he had kissed the writing on the envelope. 'My father,' he had explained and Max had seen his eyes water. He had laid the letter aside and Max, knowing how much it meant to the young man, had asked him to open and read it. 'Allah willing,' Zeyd had answered with a smile, 'there will be time when you feel you must leave.' It was then that Max had asked him whether he wished to see his wife, the Ruler having given no instructions to the contrary. Zeyd had answered immediately with an abrupt upward movement of his head. 'If there is any pay owing to me, give it to her. Allah willing, she will find another man and live in peace with the Almighty – He is the all-Forgiving.'

This was the man that Sheikh Mansour was asking his Commandant of Police to dispose of in such a way that no one need be embarrassed.

On arriving back at his bungalow home from the palace, Max poured himself a stiff whisky. He had just finished dinner when he had been called to the palace. Generally, he did not drink after dinner but this day, he judged, was an exceptional one. It is not every day the suggestion is made to a Commandant of Police that he dispose of someone in cold blood. In a lifetime of being a policeman he had performed many distasteful tasks, like directing operations for the removal in plastic bags of a hundred and twenty-six bodies from a crashed aeroplane that had lain for two days in the summer heat of the desert, or participating, because of a judge's sentence, in the hanging of a terrorist (or nationalist?) in Palestine. This, though, was different.

Sipping his whisky, Max turned over in his mind the task he was presently being invited to undertake. It contained two elements which made it hard for him to accept. First was the fact that he had formed a liking for the prisoner and considered that he had done what he had under considerable provocation. The second element was that it had simply been put to him – nothing had been committed to paper, no official ruling had been made – that it would be convenient for all concerned were the prisoner to die while in custody. Quite apart from the moral aspect – and Max was a policeman with a conscience – he was being asked to take the law into his own hands. If questions were ever asked, what could be his reply? That he was acting on the Ruler's instructions? Such a defence had an ugly ring for someone who, if not quite old enough to have taken part in the war against Nazi Germany, had nevertheless read of men pleading that the illegal acts they had committed were done on the orders of others. He could of course detail one of his men, with promises of a reward or promotion, to plunge a dagger into the prisoner's heart as he slept so that he might be at one remove from the act, but his training had taught him that it is the unpleasant tasks you perform personally and only the others that may be delegated.

Max went into the kitchen and put two water biscuits and a slice of Cheddar cheese on a plate and carried it back to the living-room. He then added some whisky to his glass and topped it up with soda. On the other hand, he argued with himself – having no one at hand to play the devil's advocate he had to perform the role himself – the circumstances of life in the sheikhdom were totally different from those obtaining elsewhere and thus different criteria must apply. After all, under sharia law, a man could have his hand chopped off for stealing or be stoned for adultery – he was pleased that Sheikh Mansour kept such punishments as deterrents and they were never put into practice. Even prison sentences were only rarely given and any foreigners found misbehaving were generally shipped back to their countries of origin. 'Why should we feed their criminals?' Sheikh Mansour would remark. There was also the argument – and the Ruler had already given it, realizing it would weigh with his Commandant of Police – that the prisoner would be spared much mental suffering if the formality of a trial followed by an execution were avoided. Would not the prisoner himself, given the choice, prefer the course of events suggested by the Ruler? Was there even not some way in which the prisoner could be given the alternative of conveniently committing suicide?

Max looked at his watch for several long seconds and was surprised to find the time a mere twenty minutes to eleven. The prisoner would have performed his final prayers and morning call was early at the prison. At this hour, therefore, the prisoner could be counted on to be deep in sleep. He rose to his feet, went into the bedroom and took the silencer from where it had lain for many years at the back of a drawer. Returning to the living-room, he fitted it to the revolver, then placed the revolver in the pocket of his cotton jacket.

He parked the Land-Rover under the tall mud walls of the building that had started life as one of the forts that the Portuguese Albuquerque had built and walked towards the iron-studded wooden gate. The guard shuffled to his feet from the bench on which he had been seated with another man and turned off the popular Egyptian song that issued from the transistor radio by his side. Having saluted, he rapped on the gate and informed his colleague inside of the Commandant's presence.

Max peered in the half-light at the man who opened the gate and recognized the fat and cheerful Abdul Wadoud, a Zanzibari who had gratefully accepted service in the local police force after several years of hard work on the decks of dhows plying between the Gulf and the East African coast.

'Give me the key to the prisoner's room.'

Abdul Wadoud handed over the key and prepared to accompany the Commandant. 'No, stay here – I shall not be long.'

Zeyd was housed in a small cell at the far end of the fort, while the rest of the prisoners, now numbering a round dozen, occupied a large room that opened directly on to the main courtyard in which Zeyd took his periods of exercise.

Max stood for a while in the open space and

looked up at an almost full moon that cast shadows from the wooden pillars that lined the far side of the courtyard. He hesitated at the door of the room, then silently inserted the key and entered. He opened the door wide and in the light provided by the small barred window he saw directly ahead of him the figure of a man at prayer. With his back to him, faced in the direction of Mecca, Zeyd was sitting with his buttocks resting on his heels and his hands on his thighs. Zeyd quickly concluded his prayers by raising his hands and passing the palms over his face.

'Is it you, sahib?'

'You should be asleep,' Max told him, and he closed the door and locked it. Walking back to the gate, he crossed the courtyard again and breathed in the night air that his lungs suddenly were hungry for. He put his hand over the revolver that hung heavy in his pocket.

'The prisoner was at his prayers,' he told Abdul Wadoud. He recollected from his studies of Islam that the very religious often performed prayers at night extra to the five daily ones enjoined on all Muslims. No doubt Zeyd's situation prompted him to spend more time in prayer.

'Is there anything for me to do?' enquired Abdul Wadoud.

Max was momentarily taken aback by the question, then recovered and answered: 'For now, there is nothing to be done, Abdul Wadoud.'

Outside, the guard scrambled to his feet and the man seated with him on the bench appeared to turn his face to one side.

Having bid them good-night, Max made his way towards the Land-Rover and drove back to his house.

Though he was tired, Max knew that sleep would elude him: too much remained unresolved and required thinking about. Never in his many years in the service of Sheikh Mansour had he been so conscious of being at a crossroads. Previously his only cause for worry had been the inevitability of having to retire from a job he enjoyed and which had become a way of life. He had no home in England, only his sister's cottage where his son spent his holidays from public school, for the boy's mother, with whom he had had a short and unsatisfactory marriage, was long since dead. During the summer months Max went back to England and he and the boy would go for holidays: with some of his schoolfriends cruising along the Severn, or fishing in Scotland, or just being together, with his sister, in the cottage. Of late, as he had grown older, the boy had joined him in the sheikhdom for Christmas and they had gone fishing on one of the Ruler's dhows or waited up at dawn at a water-hole for the flight of sand grouse. It was, he told himself, a lonely life, but that was how it had turned out and no alternative had ever presented itself. And now, was he prepared to throw it all away by resigning? Where, for one thing, would he continue to find the money for his son's expensive education?

Would it have made any difference had he found the prisoner fast asleep when he had paid his visit? Could he have brought himself to put the revolver to the man's head? Certainly he had found it impossible to do so with the man at his prayers. Though not religious, he had a certain respect (or was it envy?) for those who were.

Looking at his watch, he saw that it was past midnight. As he took the revolver from his pocket and confined it to the drawer, he knew that he would not be using it either that night or at any other time. The alternatives before him were limited to resigning his post or making whatever arrangements were required for the official execution of the prisoner.

As he walked across the room to turn off the living-room light he heard a tapping at the window. He turned off the light and walked quietly towards the sound. Looking out into the night, he saw the policeman who was on night duty at his house in the company of one of the Ruler's guards.

'Sahib,' apologized the policeman, 'I saw your light was still on and His Highness . . .'

'The Ruler wants you,' interrupted the guard. 'He is still sitting.'

'Go and tell him I am coming.'

Max closed the window and sat for some long seconds in the darkness. Never before had the Ruler summoned him at such a late hour. He sensed that the Ruler had been informed of what had happened – or had not happened – during his visit to the prison, and he brought to mind the figure of the other man seated with the guard at the gate of the fort. Was it not a face he had seen among the bandoliered ruffians at the palace?

The Ruler was in his small private *majlis* overlooking the sea. As a concession to the lateness of the hour, he wore his headscarf without the *igal* or twin strands of black twine that helped to keep it in place. It gave the Ruler a more informal, less severe mien; there was something almost benevolent in the bearded face that now looked longer and more ascetic. Max felt a sadness as the Ruler rose to his feet and they shook hands. The ritual cup of coffee was brought immediately and drunk in haste.

'And the prisoner, Mr Max,' asked the Ruler with the twist of a smile, 'did you succeed in doing as we agreed?'

'No, Your Highness,' Max answered shortly. 'With due respect I took the liberty of taking your words as a suggestion rather than an order, feeling that perhaps justice should take its course.'

'Perhaps you found you had no stomach for the task?' opined the Ruler, casting a sideways glance at his Commandant of Police. Seeing that Max remained silent, he continued: 'If you had done what we discussed it would of course have made things much easier and it would not have been necessary for us to meet at this late hour. However, I felt that maybe the matter would not be to your taste. Like me, you are a man who tries to avoid violence.' He glanced at Max quizically and then began searching in the voluminous folds of his cloak. It was only to produce his beads, and having found them he did a complete turn of them without speaking, then stared out of the window into the darkness before remarking casually: 'I have been considering the possibility of allowing the prisoner to make his escape. He could then return to his country and it would be for Allah to decide where and when he should die.'

'As Your Highness thinks best,' answered Max with, he hoped, an equally casual tone of voice. He could hardly believe his ears but, from experience, was careful not to jump to any conclusions.

'But will people believe it, Your Highness?' he found himself objecting.

The Ruler made a show of hiding a smile, then ran his fingers through his straggly salt-and-pepper beard. 'Is our prison so well guarded that no one could escape from it? Are the guards so vigilant? I suspect that Abdul Wadoud sleeps more deeply than the prisoners he is supposed to guard? Are they not open to bribery?'

'It is known that the prisoner is nothing but a

simple policeman without any money,' answered Max.

'Has he not had visitors?'

'None, May you live long. I thought it wiser for him to have no contact with the outside world.'

'No letters?' suggested the Ruler.

'The other day he received a letter from his father in Oman,' Max admitted.

'And you opened it before you gave it to him?'

Max shook his head. 'Perhaps I should have done.'

'Could it not have contained money? For all we know the prisoner's father is a wealthy merchant in the town of Muscat.' The Ruler, having made his point, smiled triumphantly at Max. 'I am merely trying to show that escaping from our fort would not be impossible.'

Max gave a nod in reply.

'And if we decide to turn a blind eye to the prisoner's escape it is only a step further to assist him in it.' The Ruler was smiling widely and clearly enjoying himself.

'And how would this be, Your Highness?' Max enquired.

'By going to the prison before daylight and bringing the prisoner out with you.'

'And the guards?' Max asked incredulously, refusing to take in the import of what the Ruler had been saying.

Sheikh Mansour shook his head slowly from side

to side as though he had suddenly found himself faced by a half-wit who was insisting on not understanding him. 'And how were you thinking – had the prisoner met his death in his cell – that you were going to persuade your guards not only to keep quiet about it but to smuggle out the body and secretly bury it?'

Unable to answer the Ruler's hypothetical question, Max gazed back into Sheikh Mansour's staring eyes.

'Now all that will be required is for the guards not to talk. There are ways of encouraging men to keep silent and other ways of discouraging them from opening their mouths.' Sheikh Mansour delved below the cushion by his side and produced two envelopes and showed Max that they contained notes. 'A small enough sum, but for such men it represents several months' pay. Tell them – am I not right that there is a certain Ahmed outside the gate and old Abdul Wadoud inside? – tell them that this money is from me personally and is payment for their silence.' He licked the flaps and banged them shut with his fist before handing them over. On the backs of the envelopes were embossed the Ruler's crest of an ornamental dagger passing across a crescent moon and the words THE RULER'S OFFICE. 'Tell them that the money comes from me personally and that the punishment for disobeying me will be swift and painful.'

'Yes, Your Highness,' said Max, folding the

envelopes and putting them in the side pocket where earlier the revolver had lain.

As though he had done all he need, the Ruler sat back and gazed at Max. 'Are you not pleased?' he asked with an enquiring smile.

'Of course, May you live long, but you have not told me how the prisoner is to make his escape, only that I should go to the prison and take him out.'

'Do not worry, I have arranged everything,' Sheikh Mansour assured him. 'So long as the silence of the guards is guaranteed you can go to the prison before dawn –' and he took out from an inside pocket a large metal watch on a chain and peered at it. 'Yes, I am afraid it will be scarcely worth your while to put your head on your pillow, but tomorrow you can sleep the whole day through. Go to the prison shortly before dawn. Take the prisoner with you in your car and leave him somewhere in one of the alleyways of the souk. From there he can make his way to the jetty. At that time of the morning there will be no one about. Tell him that all the arrangements have been made for him to return to his country. At the jetty he will find an Omani *boum* that is bound for Sohar. It will sail directly he is on board. His passage is paid. He will be landed at an Omani port and it is then up to him to make his way back home. Once that is done, Mr Max, you can go to bed knowing that our problem has been sensibly solved. Let us meet again tomorrow after sunset prayers.'

'And the dead man's relatives?' wondered Max aloud, doubts still lingering in his mind.

'I have thought of ways of compensating them,' the Ruler answered him.

'But, as we know, they want blood not money,' protested Max.

'Leave these details to me,' said the Ruler in an icy tone, indicating that he did not wish to discuss the matter further. 'You may go.'

'I give you my sincere thanks, Your Highness,' Max muttered, getting to his feet.

'Thanks are for Allah,' said the Ruler in an automatic response. 'In His hands are the heavens and the earth.'

Opening the door of the Land-Rover, Max gazed back at the black mammoth of the palace crouched against the lightening sky. Soon he saw the Ruler's *majlis* being plunged into the same darkness as the rest of the palace. He sat for a while at the steering-wheel and pondered the circumstances of his change of fortune – and those of the prisoner. Though he felt he knew the Ruler through and through, he had to admit that he was proving surprisingly unpredictable. He told himself that he should not take for granted that there were no more surprises in store for him.

Some hours later, but earlier than suggested by the

Ruler, Max returned to the fort. This time he found the guard at the gate on his own. The man rose to his feet and saluted and Max put a hand on his shoulder.

'Ahmed, I am paying another visit to the prisoner but his time I shall be taking him away with me. Do you understand?'

Ahmed succeeded in controlling his surprise. 'Yes, sahib.'

'It is not for you to know where I am taking him or for what purpose.'

'No, sahib.'

'All you have to know is that I am doing this on the orders of His Highness Sheikh Mansour. When you are asked about the events of this night and you will certainly be questioned about them by both me and others, perhaps even by the Ruler himself, as well as in the town's coffee houses – you will say that you know nothing except that I came to the prison once this night, that I paid a visit to the prisoner and that I then went away alone. Alone, you understand.'

'Yes, sahib.'

Max took from his jacket pocket one of the envelopes the Ruler had given him and held it up. 'This envelope contains a bonus for you from the Ruler himself.' The guard's hand came up to take the envelope but Max retained his hold on it. 'This is a reward for your silence. Do you understand?'

'Yes, sahib.'

'So tell me what happened tonight.'

'You came once to the prison in order to visit the prisoner, and then you went away.'

'Was there anyone with me when I left?'

'No, sahib, you were alone.'

'In this envelope is the reward for your silence. If you take the reward and yet allow your tongue to speak of tonight's true happenings, His Highness will see to it that you are put to silence for ever.'

He released his grip on the envelope and informed the man that Abdul Wadoud was going to be similarly rewarded. The guard then rapped on the gate and Max passed through into the prison.

'Once again I have come to see the prisoner,' he explained to Abdul Wadoud, 'but this time I shall be taking him out with me,' and he went through the same routine with Abdul Wadoud.

'Do not talk even with Ahmed about what has happened tonight,' he warned. 'It is a secret between the two of you, His Highness and myself.'

This time Max made no attempt to open the door to Zeyd's room noiselessly. The form in the corner under the window did not stir. Max felt his way past the table and took hold of the prisoner's shoulder and gradually tightened his grip.

'Are you not going to shoot, sahib?' Zeyd's voice spoke out of the darkness. 'I thought to make it easy for you by pretending to be asleep, for it is difficult for a man to sleep when he senses that it is his last night.'

'Allah has decreed that the time for your death has not come,' Max answered him. 'Get up – we are leaving together. Take such of your belongings as you want and come with me.'

'I have nothing I want but my father's letter and the copy of the Qur'an you gave me. Where are you taking me?'

'To safety, Allah willing.'

'Are you doing this against the Ruler's orders? I must ask you that.'

'No, don't worry, I am acting on his instructions.'

'Is there to be a trial, then?'

'No, the Ruler has decided that you should return to your own country.'

'How can that be? Why should the Ruler arrange that my life be spared? For him I am a foreigner who has killed one of his subjects and must therefore pay the price with my life. And what about the guards?'

'They have been given money for their silence.'

'And the man's relatives?' insisted Zeyd. 'Honour demands my blood.'

'That, too, the Ruler has seen to,' Max assured him.

As they walked through the courtyard towards the gate, Zeyd was clearly unable to believe the turn of events and continued to ask questions.

'And you, sahib, will you take the blame for my escape?'

Max was silent for a while before replying: 'I have not given the matter much thought. I shall have to question everyone concerned and shall presumably come to the conclusion that there was a certain degree of negligence on the part of the police and that the prisoner showed great ingenuity and daring. At least I am only obeying the orders of the Ruler himself. But let us go – we do not have all that long before it is daylight.'

The two guards saluted the Commandant of Police as he left accompanied by the prisoner.

Driving through the sparse date plantations that separated the fort from the sea coast and the township, Max realized he had left a vital question unasked.

'You can drive a car, Zeyd?'

'I was being given lessons when what happened happened. I did not take my licence, sahib.'

Max gave a laugh. 'Zeyd, I shall not rearrest you for not having a licence. I merely want to know whether you can drive this car.'

'Well enough, sahib.'

'And you know your way to the border?'

'For my first weeks as a policeman I was one of the guards at the border post.'

'Keep well inland and leave the car a mile or so from the border and cross on foot. Drive fast, for shortly after the call to dawn prayers I shall report to police headquarters that the car is missing and all border posts will automatically be put on alert. Once you reach Omani territory it will be up to you to make your way to your home town.'

'And the car, sahib?'

'If you are caught, say you stole it. Say that I had taken you from the prison and was driving you towards the souk when you succeeded in overpowering me. And leave the key in the car when you abandon it.'

The two men shook hands formally, with Max dragging his hand away as the other bent over to kiss it.

'In Allah's protection,' Max gave the traditional farewell, then added: 'And don't forget, Zeyd, that without His Highness the Ruler I would not have been able to do what I have. Do not forget him in your prayers.'

'I shall do as you say,' said Zeyd, though it was clear from his tone of voice that he remained unconvinced about the Ruler's concern for his safety.

Max watched the rear light of the Land-Rover disappear from sight down the track that led to the southern border post. In a night that was rapidly growing lighter, he wearily set off on the two-mile walk to his house.

The sentry was surprised when the Commandant of Police appeared on foot through the half-darkness. Max acknowledged his salute and walked through the garden to the house. He turned on a table lamp and slumped down in a chair. Fearful he might go to sleep where he sat, he jumped up again and went into the bedroom where he took from the dressing-table the key of the small saloon car he used when off duty. He noticed that his hand was unsteady with tiredness but his sheer curiosity demanded that he make one final sortie before enjoying the sleep the Ruler had promised him.

Dawn would soon break along the waterfront. The call to the first prayers of the day, the call that included the injunction that prayer 'is better than sleep', would soon echo out from the slender minaret of the plain whitewashed mosque that was used by the fishermen and visiting sailors. On the foreshore, alongside the different types of moored dhows, the forms of men were squatting and excreting, while on deck others pumped at primus stoves as they brewed up their heavily sweetened tea and blew out clouds of smoke from the first narghiles of the day. The smells of the waterfront mingled with those of the cargoes: spice, dried limes, fish meal exported for fertilizer and the all-pervading smell of diesel oil. Getting ready to depart was a bulky *boum* that flew the Omani flag, its deck packed with several layers of cartons bearing a little umbrella symbol and the words THIS WAY UP.

Driving slowly along the jetty, Max greeted the men on the boats till he arrived at the *boum*, the largest boat drawn up beside the jetty. The man who was clearly the boat's *naukhada* stood, with arms folded under his white untrimmed beard, a large Omani-style turban on his head.

'Peace be upon you,' Max called to him.

'And upon you be peace and the mercy of Allah and His blessings,' answered the *naukhada*.

'Travelling?' asked Max.

'If Allah wills,' answered the man.

'In the safety of Allah,' Max replied, sensing that his continued presence was an embarrassment. He then cast a quick glance beyond the *naukhada* and saw what he had expected to see: two of the Ruler's guards seated crosslegged by the engine-room, their rifles laid across their knees. As he backed out from the jetty he noticed two more guards standing in the shadow of the deserted café that faced out to sea.

With the call to prayers breaking through the silence, several men interrupted their tasks on deck and began making their way towards the mosque. The *naukhada* remained where he was, a puzzled scowl on his face.

As for Max there was nothing left for him to do but drive to police headquarters and report the theft of the Land-Rover, after which he would be free to return home to his bed.

The Ruler was in an evil mood as he sat in open *majlis* after the sunset prayers. When the Commandant of Police made his appearance one of the local merchants rose and gave up his place beside the Ruler. Max and Sheikh Mansour exchanged the necessary greetings, but when the coffee-server approached, the Ruler brusquely waved him away.

'I am told that the prisoner somehow stole the Land-Rover and drove in it towards the Omani border. Are such reports correct?' The Ruler did not wait for an answer but continued to talk in a controlled undertone so that the crowded *majlis* should not hear. 'Was it not arranged between us that you would drive the prisoner to the souk from where he would make his way to the jetty and take the boat that sailed this morning for Sohar? How can it be possible that you allowed the car to be stolen?'

'I was on the way to the souk with the prisoner as Your Highness instructed when – excuse my mentioning such a thing – I had to stop for a minute to make water...'

'Make water?' exclaimed the Ruler in a voice louder than he had intended so that several of the people waiting for an audience with him looked up in surprise.

'It was careless of me, Your Highness,' said Max in a low voice, 'but it did not occur to me that the prisoner could drive. Nothing, though, is lost, May you live long. A message was immediately sent to the border post and the Land-Rover has been recovered undamaged.'

'Well, that is certainly excellent news,' commented the Ruler, employing, for the first time to Max's knowledge, a sarcasm for which Arabs are not known.

'Thanks be to Allah,' continued Max, ignoring the Ruler's remark, 'no harm has been done and everything has turned out as Your Highness wished. All that has happened is that, while Your Highness planned for the prisoner to escape by sea, the Almighty chose that he went by land.'

'The Almighty?' queried the Ruler, his bushy brows furrowed into a deep frown. For a brief moment Max feared that he might have the unique experience of witnessing the Ruler lose his temper. Sheikh Mansour, however, quickly recovered. 'You are right, Mr Max – all has turned out for the best' – and the Ruler clapped his hands for the coffee that would terminate the meeting.

3

Open Season in Beirut

Terry Worrall humped his camera off his shoulder and rested it on the broken parquet that had once floored the entrance to one of Beirut's most expensive hotels. Thick-set, with closely cropped reddish hair streaked with grey and a thin moustache, he stood, hands on hips, and surveyed the winding staircase.

'I suppose it's too much to hope that the lifts are still working?'

The young man with the gold chain round his neck and the name NABEEL nestling in the black hair of his chest smiled back in answer.

Terry Worrall heaved up his equipment. 'Let's go,' he said.

Nabeel had been detailed to guide him to the

hotel and to see him safely through a couple of road-blocks. The previous evening the girl who called herself Joey had introduced him as her brother, but Terry wasn't convinced about that. Anyway, it didn't matter who he was so long as he knew his way about and got him to Room 814.

Terry had been in Beirut this time a mere ten days but he'd done a lot of work and made a lot of contacts and shot several thousand feet of useful material to be processed back home. He'd been into hospitals and shot sequences of doctors performing operations under primitive conditions, of mothers and fathers and wives and husbands expressing grief as no professional actor could ever do, of mass burials, of bodies being dragged around the city streets behind cars, of every possible savagery of which man is capable in a civil war. Later on would come the hours of finnicky work in the cutting-room, working all the separate bits into a coherent story, a whole that held together and could be flashed on to the world's screens. He'd be writing the commentary, too, for he reckoned that, with his various trips to Lebanon and the background reading he'd done, he was as well informed as anyone about this so-called war. He felt confident that he'd achieved as clear a picture as was possible of a war that defied being seen in terms of black and white, of Christian and Muslim or goodies and baddies; it was even difficult to determine how many sides there were, certainly more than the regulation two. He reckoned, too, that the material he'd succeeded in shooting would turn into the sort of film on which he had built his reputation in Wardour Street, a reputation that had readily produced backers to put up the money necessary for any project he had in mind. Once again he would be seen to have made a film that was informative and pulled no punches. Yet, going through his camera notes, he had felt that, comprehensive as his material was, it lacked that one outstanding sequence that would lift the whole documentary out of the rut of the merely competent. And so, last night, following up an introduction, he had succeeded, at a small bar off Hamra Street, in making the requisite contacts and arrangements.

The bargain had been struck with typical Lebanese astuteness, even down to the requirement that the fee be paid in dollars. For that he would be provided with a sequence of someone being brought down by a sniper's bullet – and the sniper would be an attractive young woman.

Some of the railing of the carpeted stairway had come away from a wall that had been pitted by gunfire, evidence of the fierce house-to-house fighting that had preceded the building's falling into the hands of the group who now occupied it and from it controlled a vital intersection of the city.

On the fifth floor Nabeel came to a stop and lit a cigarette. He didn't offer one to the Englishman, who had gruffly indicated the previous evening that he didn't use cigarettes. Terry again unshouldered the equipment, resting it on the ground beside him, the straps still held in his hand. The look on his face expressed contempt for the young man who had had to have a breather on the way up. The Englishman prided himself on many things, among them his fitness.

'Must have been quite a place,' he commented, looking along the corridor at the numbered doors stretching ahead. At the end of the corridor stood a cracked rose-coloured bath and matching bidet. A man was sitting astride the bidet, his rifle leaning against the upturned bath. He waved at Nabeel and called out something to him. Terry could tell that the man was enquiring about him. When Nabeel answered, the man said, 'Welcome,' and gave Terry an automatic smile. Nabeel crushed his cigarette underfoot and started up the stairs again. Terry shouldered the equipment and followed. At the final floor Nabeel walked to a door marked 814 directly facing the stairway, knocked and gave his name.

The door was unlocked and opened. Nabeel said something in Arabic and a woman's voice answered him. Terry passed into the room behind Nabeel. The girl who called herself Joey was in mottled battledress, with large button-down pockets on her trousers and a loose jacket. Her hair, which Terry remembered from last evening as jet black and silky, was scraped up into a peaked cap. She shifted the rifle to her left hand as she shook hands with him.

'You sure you can make your way back?' Nabeel asked him.

'Just let them know at the road-blocks that I'll be coming back later,' said Terry. 'Thanks,' he added and he took a note from his pocket and held it out to the young man.

'That's all right,' said Nabeel with a shake of his head and Terry felt he had been snubbed.

Joey and Nabeel exchanged some words in Arabic at the door. She then closed it and relocked it. The room looked spacious, being without any furniture except for the sandbags piled round the two windows overlooking the street. Terry walked to the other door across from the window, opened it and assured himself that it was a bathroom. She laughed as she watched him.

'Don't worry – no one's hiding in there,' she said.

'I wasn't worried,' he told her. 'I hardly thought you were keeping a tame boyfriend up here. It's just that I like knowing where doors lead to – a habit of mine.'

Jooey moved over to one of the mattresses that lay under the window and squatted on it. She took a packet of Chesterfield from the top pocket of her jacket, struck it against the palm of her hand and pulled one out with her lips.

'You don't,' she said.

'No, thanks.'

Beside her lay a large bowl with stub ends, also a small round cup of the sort in which Turkish coffee is served; beside it was a thermos.

'Make yourself comfortable,' she said and patted the mattress alongside her. 'Coffee?'

'Yes, I'd like some,' he said.

She unscrewed the thermos and poured dark black coffee into the cup. 'We're not used to guests up here, so you'll have to share.'

'That's fine by me.'

He left the cup on the floor and, kneeling on the mattress, peered out of the window. The buildings opposite were three or four storeys lower, with washing strung along the flat roofs. At street level the walls were battle-scarred, with windows either gaping blindly or boarded up. Slogans in flowing Arabic script were scrawled across the whitewashed walls, along with the roughly drawn picture of a man hanging from a gibbet with a balloon of Arabic issuing from his swollen tongue. One of the walls had been sliced down, displaying the entrails of a home in which people had lived and perhaps been killed. Higher up the street, near the intersection, a burnt-out car, upturned like an insect, straddled the street. Above the buildings, towards the port area and the open sea, a crooked exclamation mark of grey smoke wove itself into the blue sky.

'Not a cat to be seen,' he remarked, rising to his feet.

'Better not stand there,' she said, 'you never know

who's about. We command the street from here but occasionally some of their people hide up in the buildings opposite. Over there is enemy territory.'

He sat down uncomfortably on the mattress and sipped at the coffee. He then began unpacking his equipment.

'You may have a long wait,' she warned him.

'If we do, perhaps you'll fill in the time by telling me something about yourself. You speak English so well...'

'And French and Arabic,' she answered him. 'No doubt you want to know what a girl like me is doing in all this. I'll tell you: trying to get Beirut back to what it once was, one of the great cities of the world.'

'Well, it's hardly that now after the bashing you're all giving it. Civil wars are never pretty, but it seems that life here is about at its cheapest.'

She looked up at him and the smile she gave had little humour in it. 'You're paying the going rate,' she told him.

'So it's open season pretty well the whole year round?' he asked

She looked blankly at him.

'An expression,' he said. 'In the UK, in order to conserve the wild life, we have open and closed seasons. The open season is when you are permitted to shoot.'

'I see,' she said. 'We Lebanese have always enjoyed hunting.'

Before she stubbed out her cigarette she lit another one from it.

'I'd like as long a sequence as I can get,' he told her.

'I'll do my best,' she said. 'I can't guarantee anything – nobody's getting paid for getting killed.'

He gave a dry laugh. 'That's right,' he agreed. 'It's just the luck of the draw.'

She took up the rifle and cradled it between two sandbags. She sighted it down to the street, then turned to him. 'And I don't want any part in this film of yours – understand? That's not in the deal.'

'Fair enough,' he said, 'but the audience has got to feel that someone's doing the shooting around here. I'll just get a shot of the back of your head and your hands. You know, Joey, you've got beautiful hands and there's something terrifically sexy about hands like yours handling a gun.'

'Fine, but keep it to the beautiful hands.' She went back to looking through the sights at the street below.

'What do you do when you're not up here – like in the evenings for instance?'

'You saw,' she said. 'I sit around in bars and talk with friends about the war and all the things we're going to do when it's over.'

'But you don't drink,' he said. 'I noticed.'

'I don't care for it.'

'So what do you plan to do when it's over? – if it's ever over. The trouble with war is that after a time people become used to it, even begin to enjoy it and don't want it to stop.'

'There are also a lot of people outside who are happy for the war to go on and on,' she reminded him.

'I suppose so,' he said, then after a silence again asked her what she thought of doing after the war.

'If there's money enough maybe I'll go back to the AUB and complete my studies. Perhaps settle down and bring up a family.'

'Wouldn't that be a bit tame after all this?'

She looked sharply at him. 'I didn't choose to do this, you know. Sometimes it's just the only thing to do. You either get the hell out and jump off the boat and start a new life in Paris or somewhere or you stay and fight.'

'And with time life becomes cheaper and cheaper?'

'I suppose that's about it. We're all going to die sometime, so it's no great deal.' She laid the rifle down beside her and seated herself in the lotus position, her back against the wall. 'Some of us shoot people, Mr Worrall, and some of us pay others to shoot people so they can take pictures of it for their films.'

'That pretty well sums up what we're about,' he said with a grin, then moved closer to her on the mattress and put his hand on her shoulder. 'I asked you what you do in the evenings?'

'And I told you – sit around with friends.'

'What about sitting around with me this evening?' His hand massaged her shoulder gently.

'Are you a friend?' she asked without any coquetry.

'I'd like to be.'

'All right,' she said and removed his hand from her shoulder. 'Let's keep strictly to business,' and she uncurled her legs and knelt so as to gain a view of the street.

'Then tonight's on?' he said. 'Perhaps you can show me somewhere interesting to eat and drink, or perhaps you'd like to come and dine at the Bristol?'

'We'll see,' she said. 'I don't like planning ahead – I'm superstitious.'

'Jesus,' he said, 'you need to be if you happen to live in Beirut.'

'It's my home,' she said in a flat tone.

Again she turned her attention to the street, a cigarette burning between her fingers as she rested her head against the butt of the rifle. He had to hold himself back from stretching out his hand to caress her neck where the wisps of hair had been brushed upwards to be enclosed by the cap.

'You've got the money?' she broke the silence.

'Yes,' he said, and he unbuttoned the flap of a pocket on his jacket and produced an envelope. She took it from him and tore it open. She looked inside and made sure of the denomination of the dollar bills. 'You keep it for now,' she said, handing the envelope back, then added: 'This might be it.'

He looked over her shoulder and saw an old

man in ragged trousers and collarless shirt, his feet in slippers, appear at the gaping entrance to one of the shell-scarred buildings; he was carrying a bulging sack on his back.

Kneeling on the mattress directly behind her, he set the camera turning. He felt her tense and bring her right hand down to the trigger guard. 'Not yet,' he said urgently. 'Let's take it slowly and get as long a sequence as possible – a real "before and after" – and he panned slowly up the rubble-strewn street, held the upturned car, then came down quickly to the old man, holding him in close-up as he stood undecided in the empty doorway. The eyes in the lined, stubbled face were narrowed against the early sun's rays, then they swivelled and came to rest – perhaps attracted by a glint of light from the barrel of the gun as it rested on the sandbag – and seemed to peer in at the camera lens.

'That's great,' he muttered.

'He'll go left,' whispered the girl as though she could be overheard. 'He'll want to get to the intersection.'

'Take him just before he gets to where the car is.' He held the camera in close-up on the man's face. 'Don't let him get too far before you wing him. Just wound him first,' he instructed.

One of his knees was touching her hip and he felt her body stiffen.

'You couldn't care a shit for anyone, could you, Mr Worrall?'

'I'm in a hard business and I'm paying good money.'

Suddenly, keeping the rifle in place with her left hand, she turned round to him. 'I'd be happy to call off the deal,' she hissed.

They exchanged a long look, then he pointed down to the street. 'He's started to move.'

The old man turned out of the doorway and was skirting the wall. He limped, perhaps with the weight of the sack, perhaps because of his shapeless slippers. Nothing could be seen of him but a shuffling body with the hump of the sack twisted to one side. The shot, Terry told himself, lacked something, so, with the camera still turning, he edged back on the mattress till he was able to get her in profile, with the rifle barrel couched in the palm of her hand.

He moved forward again just in time to catch an open jeep, with armed men clinging to its side, disappear at speed towards the intersection.

As she fired, the old man shifted the sack. The force of the bullet striking the sack sent the man sprawling to the ground. He started to scramble to the safety of an open doorway, then the second bullet struck him high up on the shoulder. He squirmed round, a hand clasped to his shoulder, blood seeping through the fingers. The expression on his face was a mixture of surprise and pain, though his other hand reached out for the sack. Then, having decided to abandon the sack, he began crawling on all fours along the pavement in a frantic attempt to cover the few yards to safety.

'Hold it!' Terry said urgently as he crouched above her, supporting himself against the wall as his arms began to tire.

When the old man reached the open doorway, Terry muttered tensely: 'Finish him off with one to the head.'

The shot splattered the man's brains against the whitewashed wall as his body slumped to the pavement. The camera continued its steady whirr against the silence of which the two of them were now all at once conscious.

He let out a sigh of satisfaction, almost of relief and brought the camera to his side. He felt drained as though he had just performed an act of sex.

'It couldn't have been better,' he said. 'I got some great shots. Thanks.'

As he took up the camera and unscrewed the telescopic lens, Joey carefully rested the rifle against one of the sandbags. Leaning her back against the wall, she watched him in silence. 'It's funny using the same word "shoot" about a camera,' she said as though to herself.

He smiled at her. 'We're pretty well in the same business.' He noticed that she looked pale and strained. 'You were great,' he said, hoping she would return his smile.

'Can I have the money now?'

'Of course,' he said and he took the envelope

from his pocket. Then he shouldered his camera and smiled down at her. 'Bye – and don't forget this evening. I'll see myself out.'

'I like to have the door locked,' she said, getting to her feet and taking up the rifle.

At the door he held out his hand to her. 'Thanks, Joey.' She shifted the rifle to her left hand. She gave no answering squeeze to his handshake. 'See you,' he said.

He turned at the top of the stairs and waved to her. At the next landing he glanced upwards at the sound of her voice. 'Mr Worrall?'

'Yes, Joey?'

She was standing at the top of the stairway. 'Sorry, tonight's not on.'

'But I thought we'd ...' As in slow motion he saw her raise the rifle. The bulky equipment slowed his reaction. He tried to throw himself sideways towards the stair-rail, but the bullet ripped into his neck. He lay on his back staring up at her with a look of disbelief on his face and waited for the next bullet.

4
Slice of the Cake

Apart from the fact that the minister kept mispronouncing his name, Martin Eagleton was satisfied that the meeting had gone well. His friend the deputy minister had warned him that he would find the minister, if he ever got to meet him, a somewhat formidable character who had been appointed to his present post by the president because of his past performances on the field of battle. He had not expected to meet the minister at all, the negotiations having been carried out with Mahmoud Abdul Sattar, the deputy minister, and the various technical men in the ministry. It was only because Mahmoud had been sent off on some important assignment a couple of days ago that he had received a message at the hotel that the minister himself would like to meet him. It was really quite an honour, though more of a courtesy call, all the specifications, prices and delivery dates having already been agreed.

The minister's office was impressive, with its large uncluttered desk and the life-size portrait of the president in informal battledress looking, as it were, over the minister's shoulder. They had both been military men and had risked their lives in the coup that had brought the president to power, and they both had the same conformation of jaw and the same thick eyebrows and full moustache. The minister's knowledge of English was adequate but basic – not like his deputy who had acquired fluency together with a Yorkshire accent when graduating from a technical college in the north of England. Now, standing beside the large desk, was a young assistant in suit and tie and with a degree in English literature from the local university.

'As you know, Mr Eagleton,' explained the assistant, 'Mr Mahmoud is away at present on urgent business. However, His Excellency felt that he would like to meet the man with whom we have been negotiating such an important contract.'

'I am most honoured, Your Excellency.' Martin Eagleton turned to the minister with a decorous smile. 'It has been a great pleasure to do business with yourselves and your very efficient staff.'

'In this country we like to be correct,' said the minister, making a chopping movement with his right hand. The minister then turned to his assistant and they exchanged some words in Arabic.

'His Excellency says that we have been hearing from your friend Mr Mahmoud how difficult it was to arrive at a price that was agreeable to both sides,' said the assistant.

'Mr Mahmoud, Your Excellency, is a very skilful negotiator,' said Martin Eagleton with a histrionic movement of both hands. 'As we say in English, he has the interests of the ministry at heart.'

The assistant translated to the minister, who smiled at the Englishman in front of him, then once again spoke through his assistant.

'His Excellency is sure that the result will be good for all parties. He is also hopeful that everything will be concluded right away. In this country we do not like to waste time.'

'Would it be in order, seeing that everything has been agreed and that the contract merely requires Your Excellency's signature, if I were to book out on a plane tomorrow?' Martin Eagleton enquired.

The minister, making sure he had understood correctly, leaned towards his assistant, then spread out his large hands on the desk.

'You no like our country, Mr Eggleton? You no like eat more of our kebab?' – and the three men laughed heartily.

The minister suddenly looked serious as he consulted his gold watch. He tapped the face as he exchanged words with his assistant.

'His Excellency suggests that you take a plane out tomorrow afternoon,' said the assistant.

'Can everything be concluded by then?' asked Martin Eagleton, unable to disguise the surprise in his voice. He had already made up his mind that he might well have to stay on a further week or so before he finally got the contract signed. At one time it had seemed that the negotiations would go on for ever with endless hair-splitting by the government officials. Anyone would think the powers-that-be had a financial interest in keeping the capital's hotels filled with overseas company representatives. Once again it had been Mahmoud, the deputy minister, who had got the negotiations moving along the right lines.

'*Inshallah*,' said the minister, wagging a finger at him and laughing. 'You know you must always say *inshallah* about the future. Only He knows for certain' – and the minister pointed upwards with a lifting of the head.

'*Inshallah*,' said Martin Eagleton, exaggerating the pronunciation.

'Excellent!' acclaimed the minister, and the three men again laughed heartily.

Then the minister stood up and he and Martin Eagleton shook hands across the desk, after which the assistant saw him to the door and even accompanied him out into the street to help him find a taxi.

Arriving back at the hotel, he found a new man

on duty at the desk. He had to give him his name and room number before being handed his key.

'You are checking out tomorrow, Mr Eagleton?' the man asked.

'I never said so,' he answered curtly.

'We were told you would be leaving tomorrow.'

He was irritated at the thought that someone from the ministry had obviously already told the hotel when he would be leaving. What further irritated him was that he was now informed that for his final night at the hotel they were arranging for him to occupy another room. The man at the desk then went into a garbled story to the effect that he had informed them that he was leaving today and his room had already been promised to a gentleman from Germany who had specially requested that particular room. When he began protesting that he had no intention of vacating the room he had occupied during the last sixteen days, the man apologized and told him that unfortunately his belongings had already been packed into his suitcases and moved to another room. The new room was similar to the one he had been occupying, in fact was more spacious and better furnished and was equipped with a wide-screen TV set. While more expensive than his present room, he was told that, because of any inconvenience he had suffered, he would be charged the same price.

Though enraged at the high-handed way he had

been dealt with, he told himself that nothing was to be gained by kicking up a fuss. These were not battles that one won; were not in fact battles worth engaging in. He had worked long enough in the Arab world to know that you had to learn to be philosophical about much of what went on.

He went into the bar, ordered a beer and comforted himself with the thought that this was his last night in the place and that tomorrow he would be sitting in a plane with a contract in his pocket. He then went upstairs to his new room. He noted that it was in fact a larger room and was more comfortably furnished. He also saw the new outsize TV. He was conscious of the slight hum of traffic penetrating through the curtains. He pulled them aside and saw that his room faced a corner of the capital's main square. He shrugged his shoulders – by the time he had had a few more beers he would be immune to all traffic noises.

He decided to go out and have lunch, then be available at the hotel for the afternoon should he be required at the ministry. He ate a plate of kebab and rice at a fraction of the price the hotel would have charged, then returned to the hotel for another beer.

'I'm expecting an important call from the ministry,' he told the man at the desk.

Upstairs, having removed his coat and tie and kicked off his shoes, he settled down in one of the two armchairs to watch a repeat of a football match from a stadium in Spain, complete with a raucous commentary in Arabic. With the sound turned off, he fell into a deep sleep from which he was woken by the ringing of the telephone. When he answered it, he heard the voice of a woman speaking in Arabic. He listened for several seconds, then put the receiver down.

At the desk he told them that he had had a wrong number, some woman talking in Arabic, but the man tried to tell him that the call was for him. It was now cool and he went outside and walked to the airline office to book himself out the following day. He was surprised to find that a booking had already been made in his name on the afternoon plane. He handed over his ticket and had the flight number and date marked in.

The evening lay uncomfortably empty ahead of him. Spending free time on one's own in hotel bedrooms was, however, all part of being an overseas representative. You filled the hours with daydreaming, writing letters back home and reading the paperback thrillers you had bought at Heathrow. There was also, of course, the temptation to drink oneself into a daze. At least, he assured himself, this was his last evening in the place. He would have liked to be able to spend it with Mahmoud on a celebratory spree. It would have been fun to go off to one of those little garden restaurants where they served bottles of the local arak, the kind made of dates rather than the Lebanese variety which was made of grapes. While the local arak had a kick of its own it left you with a mighty hangover the next morning but you soon got used to that. As a deputy minister and someone who enjoyed the good life, Mahmoud was well known and was given special attention in the city's bars and restaurants, which included being given a discreet corner table out of sight of other customers. However, as he told his English friend, it was wise for the two of them not to be seen too much together, also that Martin should not try ringing him at home. As it happened, there was no necessity for them to meet up as there was nothing more to discuss. He had the number of Mahmoud's account at the bank in Zurich and he would get the company to send off his commission as and when payments were received from the government. In such arrangements there had to be complete trust; no way could anything be committed to writing. He was confident that Mahmoud too could be trusted, that when he made his yearly trip to Europe in the summer he would find his own half of the commission paid into an account he was planning to open in Geneva. What better arrangement, from everyone's point of view, than to have the relevant deputy minister with a slice of the cake? It was amusing to think that he himself would also be earning himself a pat on the back from his sales director, perhaps hopefully a rise in salary and even a bonus cheque.

Bored with the television, he went downstairs

and persuaded the man at the bar to let him have — at a price — a quarter-bottle of Scotch. Back in his room, he turned the television on again and watched a thriller about someone without a gun being chased round the streets of Helsinki by someone with one. While he watched he allowed his mind to wander among the names of places such as Cannes, Antibes and Cap Ferrat. He decided he must make a trip to the South of France, maybe with his wife, to see what was on offer. On the other hand, property was likely to be cheaper in Spain, perhaps in Majorca, or why not somewhere like Paphos in the Greek part of Cyprus, which was conveniently halfway between his stamping grounds and the UK. In the meantime, while he was looking for some whitewashed villa with a small garden, the money could be earning him interest. The thriller came to an end and he found himself watching with increasing boredom a domestic Arabic comedy filmed in Cairo. He turned down the sound and amused himself by taking down his jacket from the back of the door and extracting an old envelope from the inside pocket. He scribbled on to it some figures, a series of percentages and likely dates for payment. It was a calculation he had done before but it gave him pleasure to do the arithmetic and to gaze at the substantial total he would be making for himself. He then tore up the envelope and went to the bathroom and threw the pieces into the lavatory bowl; he had to flush it twice before all evidence of his sums had disappeared.

He had a heavy and indifferent meal in the hotel restaurant accompanied by two more beers and sat on for a while listening to a three-man band playing tunes that were favourites before he was born. On the way up to the room he stopped at the desk and ordered a continental breakfast with coffee in his room at nine o'clock. When the man handed him an envelope, he frowned and told him that he should have let him know directly it arrived.

'It's an important letter from the ministry. For heaven's sake, I was next door in the restaurant,' he snapped.

He was becoming increasingly irritated with the people at the desk.

'It only just came, sir – it was delivered by hand.'

'I know, I know,' he said impatiently and gave an upwards lift of his eyebrows to register his dissatisfaction.

He waited till he was in his room before opening the envelope. Through the haze of the several beers he registered that the contents of the envelope were quite clearly not those of a contract. Instead, he took out a single sheet of paper and read:

DEAR MR EAGLETON,
This is to inform you that it has been decided not to proceed with the negotiations in which

this Ministry was engaged with your good selves. At the same time we have written to your company in England informing them that their name has been removed from the list of companies qualified to compete for government tenders.

The letter was written on ministry paper and had a scrawl for a signature under the words 'For H.E. THE MINISTER'.

He read the letter through a second time, unable to believe its brusque contents. Only that morning he and the minister himself had been sharing jokes. What had gone wrong?

His heart beat fiercely against his ribcage. A surge of annoyance at Mahmoud mounted from deep inside him. Where was the man? How could he leave him on his own at such a time? It was up to him to get the whole thing back on the rails. Failing intervention by Mahmoud, should he himself seek another meeting with the minister?

As he sat back and tried to clear his head, his feeling of annoyance and frustration turned to one of unease. It seemed that a letter had already been sent to his company, so there was no rescuing the situation. What possible story could he tell his company, which had already been informed by him that the contract was in the bag?

'Where the hell was Mahmoud?' he asked himself, emptying out the rest of the whisky.

He swallowed it down in one gulp and made his way unsteadily to the large bed where his pyjamas were neatly folded on the pillow. Despite his worries, he fell asleep immediately.

He was awakened by the strident sound of an approaching siren. At the same time there was a knock at the door and a breakfast trolley was wheeled in.

'What time is it?' he asked the waiter. The man appeared not to have heard him as he went to the curtains covering the large expanse of glass and drew them back. The funereal light of early dawn seeped into the room. It was, he realized, considerably earlier than the time at which he had ordered breakfast. What were the people at reception up to now?

As he made his way to the bathroom, he was reminded of yesterday's letter from the ministry. A ball of foreboding lodged itself inside his chest, bringing on a sensation of tightness. He stopped and glanced towards the window. He saw a gathering of people waiting in the half-light. They watched as the back door of an ambulance was opened and a man, barefoot and dressed in what looked like a sewn-up sheet, was helped out by two uniformed figures. They half led, half carried him up the wooden steps of a platform. A third uniformed man awaited him at the top of the steps and passed a large placard with Arabic writing over his head so that it rested on his chest. Martin

Eagleton scarcely recognized in the sunken features his dapper friend the deputy minister. For a second it seemed that Mahmoud's staring eyes met his own before the dangling rope was secured round the bared neck.

5
Deal Concluded

Two days previously Colonel Gray, one of HMG's arms salesmen from the MoD, had flown in to the self-imposed austerity and indigenous heat and humidity of a small Gulf sheikhdom. Though summoned by the Ruler, he had been kept kicking his heels for a whole day and a morning in the hotel before being granted a meeting. Now, as the *muezzin* from the palace mosque gave the call to sunset prayers, Colonel Gray disconsolately descended the marble steps, opened the door of the taxi he had waiting for him and told the driver to take him back to the hotel.

Colonel Gray had known Emil at Reception for many years and found no difficulty, with the help of a ten-dollar bill, in persuading him to have a small teapot of whisky sent up to his room. He then asked Emil to get him the airline office on the phone and booked himself in on tomorrow's flight to London. 'No – tourist,' he said tersely and felt a stab of resentment at the thought of the many reps in the area, selling anything from toothbrushes to prefabs, who received first-class tickets from their companies. He then sent back a fax to the MoD informing them of his imminent return. In order to prepare them for the worst – when they were expecting him to come back with a contract in his pocket – he ended with the words: 'Negotiations proceeding highest level but unforeseen difficulties likely demand further visit.' He described it to himself as a 'holding' manoeuvre while he racked his brains to think of the least damaging way of breaking the bad news.

The meeting he had just had with the Ruler had been a disaster. During the two years of Colonel Grays's toing and froing between London and the Arabian Gulf the Ruler had alternated between increasing the order dramatically and slashing it drastically, whilst constantly whittling away at the prices.

So taken aback had Colonel Gray been when informed that the deal was off that he had found his voice turning into a high-pitched squeak of disbelief as he asked the interpreter: 'Does His Highness mean he doesn't want any of this?' – and he had pointed with a stubby finger at the beautifully prepared contracts, expensively bound and awaiting signature, that lay on the table between himself and the Ruler.

The interpreter had translated to the Ruler and the answer was fired back, stark and unvarnished: 'Not a single bullet.'

Colonel Gray had flashed a glance at the Ruler in the hope that His Highness might be joking – Colonel Gray prided himself on having developed an informal man-to-man relationship with the Ruler – but the latter was wholly engrossed in examining what looked like an oversized emerald in the cufflinks that fastened the sleeve of his gown. There had obviously been nothing to be done but say his farewells and collect up the volumes of offers for Britain's latest early-warning system, ground-to-air missiles and a fleet of torpedo boats.

Before leaving London this time he had been informed that the final total figure of one hundred and thirty-three million pounds could not be negotiated and didn't have an ounce of fat on it. Had it not been for the size of the deal and the fact that England's factories were desperate for work, he'd have been told long ago to forgo any further trips to this particular Arabian Gulf sheikhdom. The general, head of MoD sales, had more than once made the damnfool remark to him about airline tickets not growing on trees; he had also reminded him about the vast amount of costly paperwork that was constantly having to be redone and the way in which Colonel Gray was being forced to make more and more price-cuts and concessions about delivery dates, maintenance back-up, free training courses and performance guarantees.

He took the lift upstairs to his room where he found the pot of tea, a tea cup and a bottle of iced mineral water. He spluttered down his regimental tie with the first mouthful of whisky and wondered if it wasn't some kind of home brew of Emil's, whether in fact he wouldn't have been wiser to have waited till he boarded tomorrow's plane before trying to drown his sorrows.

What possible, or impossible, story could he think up for London? How to explain that HH had suddenly appeared to change his mind after all these months of negotiations? It almost looked as if HH were engaged in a personal vendetta against him and the MoD. Could he tell London that political pressure had been put on HH to buy French equipment; that the French had suddenly come up with a soft loan if he bought from them? That HH had, on the spur of the moment, decided to disband his army, navy and airforce? That highly confidential information had been leaked to him, that... that...

The phone by the bed rang. His heart sank as it occurred to him it might be London ringing to enquire. He rose unsteadily and seated himself on the bed. Only now did he realize how tired he was, that there was a lot to be said for taking his pension and devoting himself to keeping the lawn in trim at his suburban Surrey house.

'Gray,' he said, in the tone of a man giving a résumé of an English weather report.

'This is Mr Saad Labeeb,' said the voice at the other end. 'I am speaking with Colonel Gray? Excellent... Colonel Gray, I would be grateful to have five minutes of your precious time.'

He felt like answering that there was little that was precious about his time at present, but replied coolly, 'I'm sorry but I'm leaving first thing in the morning.'

'I know,' said Mr Labeeb. 'You are booked on the early plane to London, but I don't think you should leave before we have had the opportunity of a chat, colonel.'

He would have preferred to have spent the evening on his own, temporarily escaping from his worries in Emil's evil-tasting brew, and then having an early night, but he had learnt that in business one should never refuse to hear what someone had to say.

'Listening's the one thing that doesn't cost a bean,' he used to tell his cronies at the local with a sage purse of his lips. He therefore informed Mr Labeeb, who had explained he was talking from Reception, that he'd be right down.

He swallowed his drink with a grimace, hid the teapot in the bedside cupboard and took the stairs down to the lobby.

The man standing by the desk was young, by the colonel's standards, with sleek black hair and an uncomfortable weight of gold round his wrists, on his fingers and dangling from his neck. He wore a suit of shot silk in dove grey, a large tie that advertised the maker's name, and narrow shoes made from some expensive reptile's skin.

'Mr Labeeb?' the colonel asked unnecessarily, the lobby being otherwise deserted.

The two men shook hands. Colonel Gray was famed for his painful manly grip, but Mr Labeeb managed to escape from it unharmed. Giving the colonel a crocodile's smile, he took him by the elbow, as though they had been friends since preparatory-school days, and guided him towards the lounge. As he did so he called back to Emil in Arabic. Colonel Gray knew sufficient of the language, picked up in the bars of hotels throughout the Middle East, to recognize the word for ice and the lingua franca of 'Coca-Cola'. His feelings of antagonism towards Mr Saad Labeeb increased still further: he didn't like being told what he should drink and, with the limited choice available, would have much preferred a Turkish coffee.

'What can I do for you?' he asked the Lebanese stonily, as the latter selected a corner of the lounge and sat down.

'I think it's more a question of what I can do for you, colonel,' Mr Labeeb answered, '– or perhaps I should say what we can do for each other.'

The Coca-Colas were brought in tall frosted glasses with slices of lemon. Mr Labeeb raised his glass and said, 'Cheers.' Pretending not to have heard, Colonel Gray sipped at his drink with distaste, then brightened up as he found it to be a totally different form of Coke from any he had known.

'Emil always freshens it up for me with a generous helping of Bacardi rum,' Mr Labeeb explained, then sat back in his armchair and crossed his legs, one reptilian shoe brushing against the colonel's trousers.

'I was very sorry to learn that His Highness did not sign the contract with you this afternoon.'

Colonel Gray played it with as much sang froid as he could summon up. 'Yes, I suppose it'll mean yet another visit,' he remarked wryly, lifting his glass to his lips and giving Mr Labeeb a quick sideways look. He reminded himself that interpreters in this part of the world increase their income substantially by passing on information to third parties. How much, though, did Mr Labeeb in fact know of his meeting with the Ruler?

'I understand His Highness indicated that he had no intention of signing the contract,' said Mr Labeeb and began rattling the ice cubes in his glass in an irritating manner.

'Oh, I wouldn't put it quite like that,' retorted the colonel, feeling himself on the retreat. He sipped at his glass and glowered. 'Anyway, might I ask what it has to do with you, Mr Labeeb?'

'For the moment, nothing,' Mr Labeeb admitted, showing his immaculate teeth.

'I presume you learnt of my conversation with His Highness from the interpreter?'

'From Ahmed Nejm? Good heavens, no!' – and he uncrossed his legs and doubled up with laughter.

'Then maybe from His Highness himself?' suggested the colonel with heavy sarcasm.

'Just so.' He glanced at the colonel approvingly.

'Of course, you're a friend of the Ruler's,' the colonel continued in the same tone.

'That is so,' Mr Labeeb confirmed.

'I might have known,' said Colonel Gray, seeming to make an effort to suppress a laugh. He then produced a bright red handkerchief from his sleeve with the air of a conjurer about to perform his last and best trick and noisily blew his nose.

'I see, colonel,' said Mr Labeeb, 'that you remain unconvinced about my ability to help you.' Then, leaning forward and speaking in a low voice, he provided the colonel with precise details of the deal that the MoD had for so long been trying to conclude with the Ruler. He ended up by mentioning the sum of one hundred and thirty-three million pounds.

Colonel Gray endeavoured to look unimpressed at Mr Labeeb's extensive knowledge of the proposed deal, knowledge that could have been gained only from the Ruler himself.

'May I take it, Mr Labeeb, you are suggesting that for a modest fee you will use your influence to try and obtain this contract for us?'

Colonel Gray knew his Lebanese middlemen. What this particular one did not seem to realize was that all the influence in the world couldn't pull this one out of the fire.

'No, no, I am not looking for a modest fee for *trying* to get you the contract, I am asking for a modest percentage for actually getting you it. I am a man who works only on results, colonel – no results, no percentage. Could anything be fairer than that?'

The colonel pointed out that it was well known that His Highness did not approve of agents or middlemen, holding the view that money paid out to them was money paid out of his own coffers.

For answer the Lebanese middleman looked at his paper-thin gold watch with undisguised impatience and gave a theatrical shrug of his well-padded shoulders.

'You are a free man, my dear sir. May I, though, ask you just one simple question: if, as we both know, His Highness showed no interest in signing the contract and did not even ask for further cuts in your prices...'

'Further cuts?' groaned Colonel Gray. 'Any further cuts and we'd be into national bankruptcy.'

The other flashed a look of irritation at having been interrupted. 'If, as I was saying, there is no hope of the contract being signed, what have you to lose by cooperating with me?'

There was, Colonel Gray had to admit to himself, something in what the fellow was saying.

'What *have* I to lose, Mr Labeeb?' he asked, attempting the impossible task of looking him in the eye.

'A mere half per cent – payable pro rata as and when payments are made to your government.'

As a matter of habit Colonel Gray looked shocked whenever commission percentages were mentioned. In vain he tried to work out in his head the sum involved. 'But that's ... that's ...'

'It would mean a commission of six hundred and sixty-five thousand pounds – not a large sum where a hundred and thirty-three million is concerned.' He lifted a well-manicured hand as the colonel was about to protest. 'Yes, I know you must ring London before you can agree to any such arrangement.' He looked at his watch and added, 'You'll just about catch them – it's coming up to midnight there.'

'There's not a ghost of a chance they'll agree,' said Colonel Gray testily. The thought of calling the general at this hour was daunting – and it wasn't as if he'd got any good news to impart. Wouldn't he be merely making matters worse for himself by giving London further false hopes? 'Anyway, I'm afraid it's all too late in the day now. We'd have to sit down and work out an agreement and I'm off first thing tomorrow.'

'For the moment you are, colonel, but I would suggest, after all the work you've put into it, that a further night's stay would be justified. As for the agreement, I have it here all typed out and ready for signature. You will see that under the agreement I am giving myself a mere twenty-four hours in which to procure you the Ruler's signature to the contract.'

He took from his breast pocket a long beige envelope from which he extracted two copies of an agreement that began '*Whereas the parties . . .*'

Half an hour later, with Mr Labeeb's help – it came as no surprise to learn that he happened to know the man in charge of international calls – the colonel was back in his room talking to an irate general, who had clearly either been woken from sleep or been interrupted in his efforts to get up the necessary steam for his weekly manoeuvres with Mrs General. 'Ring me any time of the day or night,' Colonel Gray remembered the general telling him when he'd joined 'the firm' several years back – and what could be more important than a contract for a hundred and thirty-three million pounds?

'You really must get it into your head, old man, when we tell you we can't knock another penny piece off the bill . . . Yes, I know, I know, but every damned time you see your good friend the Ruler you're giving more of our money away . . . My dear chap, who are you working for, him or us? . . .

Another half per cent before, with any luck, you can get him to sign? Out of the question. After all, that's ... that's ...' Colonel Gray was able to supply his superior with the exact sum that would be lost to the British government if a further half per cent were deducted. 'And what's all this "with any luck"? You want us to agree to give away another half per cent and even then we need "luck"' – and his tone of voice underlined the word heavily – 'before we're going to be allowed to sign this disastrous contract?' Colonel Gray gritted his teeth and provided the general with the information that the percentage represented an agent's commission. This brought an explosion from his chief. 'But look here, Gray, you've always made us believe that HH wouldn't countenance any middlemen, that it was the one country in the Middle East ... Yes, I'm perfectly aware we're on an open line but this is no time for beating about the bush ... Well, I suppose if you must you must, but don't expect any red carpets when you get back ... This contract's a real calamity and has been from the moment you first put foot in that palace ... All right, then, sign him up for a half per cent and give him twenty-four hours, and God help you – God help us all – if you don't come back with the contract ...'

On his return to the lounge, he was grateful to find that Mr Labeeb had ordered two more Coca-Colas.

'Got the green light all right? Jolly good.' He had

the papers spread out on the table in front of him. Colonel Gray nodded sourly, took up one of the copies and read it through twice, then checked that the other pages were an exact copy. He signed both copies and handed one to Mr Labeeb, who rewarded him with one of his widest saurian smiles.

'Tomorrow, *inshallah*' – and he pronounced the word in broken Arabic for the colonel's benefit – 'you will have your contract signed by His Highness.'

'I'll believe it when I see it.' He rose to his feet abruptly, suddenly the man of action. 'If you'll excuse me, Mr Labeeb, I'll be saying good–night. You see, I've got to arrange to keep on my room, also to cancel my flight tomorrow.'

'No problem, colonel. Everything has been taken care of.'

The following morning he was summoned to the palace where an unusually affable Ruler received him. As though it were the most normal thing in the world for someone to change his mind so abruptly from one day to the next, His Highness signed the thick volume of pages that formed the contract between himself and the British Ministry of Defence. On returning to the hotel, Colonel Gray sent a fax to London: 'Deal concluded. Flying Athens tomorrow and thence London on Friday. Regards Gray.'

Though his presence in Athens was in no way

necessary — he had sowed the seeds back at the office that Athens had now replaced Beirut as the place in which to make contacts — he always enjoyed a night or two there at the Hilton. He was in any case in no hurry to get back to the office and a quiet weekend at home would help him work out the line he'd take with the general on Monday.

With a temperature only a degree or two less hot than the Arabian Gulf, Athens none the less was in many ways agreeably different. During the long drive in from the airport he decided how he'd spend his evening: he'd bath, have a haircut (they could put it down on his bill), then he'd go into the bar and have one of their excellent Bloody Marys, or perhaps two, and then take himself out to one of those *tavernas* where they played *bouzouki* music, danced and broke plates.

No sooner had he entered the bar and been greeted by one of the waiters than he was spotted by Jerry Wagstaff-Jones, one of the people 'in the business' whom he liked less than somewhat. Jones, as he preferred to think of him, was sitting on his own and it would have been churlish not to join him. Wagstaff-Jones was the Middle East rep for a Belgian company that made an inferior night-sight which, by dint of generous backhanders, he sold in vast quantities throughout the Arab world, as though it were an article that no self-respecting family could be without. That Wagstaff-Jones was one of his particular *bêtes noires* was due to his being reported as having once said about MoD salesmen that all they had up their sleeves were grubby handkerchiefs. This, though, had not stopped the colonel from continuing to house his handkerchief in his sleeve.

Colonel Gray said he'd like a Bloody Mary and told the waiter to see it came with plenty of pepper in it.

'How's biz?' said Jerry Wagstaff-Jones, who was drinking malt whisky on the rocks.

'Can't complain. And you?'

'Couldn't be better,' said Wagstaff-Jones, taking up a handful of pistachio nuts from the bowl in front of them.

'Just arrived?' asked Wagstaff-Jones.

'A couple of hours ago,' said the colonel.

'From the Gulf?' suggested Wagstaff-Jones.

'Cairo,' said the Colonel, who never believed in revealing his movements. As he saw Wagstaff-Jones open his mouth to ask a further question, he added: 'Good to be back in Athens, I must say.'

'Lovely people the Greeks,' said Wagstaff-Jones. 'Better grub here too.'

'That's right,' said the colonel, grabbing a handful of pistachio nuts while he could and lifting his Bloody Mary straight from the waiter's tray to his mouth.

Wagstaff-Jones ordered himself another drink, then motioned the colonel nearer: Heard the one about the Yanks who wanted someone for a manned flight to Jupiter?'

'No,' said the colonel, who was hoping to tell the one about the Irishman whose greyhound had gone lame.

'Well, the Yanks were all ready with their spaceship for Jupiter but reckoned it was too dangerous for one of their own chaps, so asked for volunteers. An Englishman, a Frenchman and a Lebanese applied, and when the Englishman was asked how much he wanted he said one million . . .'

'One million dollars?' enquired the colonel.

'Dollars . . . pounds,' said Wagstaff-Jones, annoyed by the interruption. 'When the Yanks asked him why he wanted so much, the Englishman said he didn't reckon his chances of coming back were all that good and he wanted to provide for his wife. When the Frenchman was asked how much he wanted he said *two* million and the Yanks asked why two million and the Frenchman said he didn't reckon his chances of coming back alive were too good and he had a wife and a mistress to provide for – a million a piece.'

'And the third guy, the Lebanese?' prompted the colonel, trying desperately to bring to mind the punchline of the story of the Irishman and the lame greyhound.

'So in goes the third applicant, the Lebanese. When he's asked how much he'd want to go to

Jupiter, he says, 'Three million.' 'Three million,' say the Yanks, 'how do you work that out?' 'Well,' says the Lebanese, 'we've got to have one million for the Englishman who'll be going in the spacecraft and then there's one million for me and one million for you.' And guess who gets the contract? The Lebanese!' and Wagstaff-Jones almost choked himself as he laughed and tried to swallow a pistachio nut simultaneously.

Colonel Gray was pouring the dregs of his first Bloody Mary into his newly arrived second when he became aware of somebody standing in the doorway of the bar and scanning the various tables. With horror he recognized Saad Labeeb who must, he realized, have been up front in the first class of the same plane. If there's one thing that gives an arms salesman goose pimples, it's meeting one of his contacts when in the company of another arms salesman. Racking his brains as to how to introduce Saad Labeeb if necessary, or whether to pretend that he had been mistaken for someone else, the colonel saw with relief the Lebanese pass by their table and walk to the bar. He drank deeply to his good fortune (or was it the middleman's discretion?), then heard his companion remark: 'You know Saad, of course?'

He looked up vaguely and squinted his eyes in the direction of Saad Labeeb's back. 'Can't say that I do,' he said.

'But you must,' protested Wagstaff-Jones —

'Lebanese chappie who used to operate out of Beirut. Could always be found in the bar at the Vendôme. Very smooth customer – just the sort to be able to pocket a million and never go anywhere near a spaceship.'

'Wouldn't be in our line of business, would he?'

'Not really. Friend Saad wouldn't know the difference between a heat-seeker and a flying carpet.' Wagstaff-Jones chortled at his joke, a trusty standby he used to effect about a lot of people.

'Is that so?'

'Which doesn't stop him making a lot of money out of arms, or anything else for that matter, and every penny piece is made in –' and he mentioned the sheikhdom from which Colonel Gray had just come.

'Oh yes?' said Colonel Gray nonchalantly.

'He and HH have a great little ploy they engage in once in a while. If there's a likely deal coming to a head the Ruler puts through a call to Athens and gets Saad out on the next plane. In the meantime HH has been playing silly buggers with some poor rep who's being driven out of his senses by his demands for a bit off here and a bit off there...'

Colonel Gray took a long gulp from his Bloody Mary.

'When HH reckons he's pared everything down to the bone and the poor bloody rep's been haring back and forth to the UK – or wherever – getting himself more deeply into the doghouse with his boss back home, HH suddenly asks for him pronto. Everyone presumes that at long last the contract's going to be signed and the rep's taking the palace steps two at a time, only to be told by HH that after all he's decided he doesn't want the stuff. If the rep in desperation makes some further cut in his prices, HH pretends to accept, but then again refuses to sign on the dotted line. At this stage in the proceedings, enters friend Saad Labeeb in his golden armour and with an outsize halo round his head. He promises to rescue the position for a very modest commission, because of course by that time there's not much meat left on the bone.'

'But at least he lands a deal that would otherwise be lost?' the colonel suggested with studied casualness.

'Oh, he lands the deal all right because the deal's in the bag in any case. By that time the Ruler's made up his mind to go through with the deal. Having got every cent he can off the price he sends friend Saad in to bat. From their point of view there's nothing to lose. If Saad succeeds with some sucker to get himself signed up for a quarter per cent, that's fine and he and the Ruler split the commission – and Saad has his ways of repaying such little favours. If the rep won't play, then the Ruler just goes ahead and signs the contract as it is and he and Saad try their ploy in another deal.'

The colonel downed his drink and signalled to a passing waiter: 'Same again.' Colonel Gray felt his mind was not as sharp as it should have been to take in what he had just been told. Speaking slowly and more thickly than he would have wished, he recapitulated:

'What you're saying is that when our friend over there hoves onto the horizon it's a sure sign that HH is about to sign on the dotted line. All you have to do is to play it cool with HH and reject our friend's blandishments and you've saved yourself his commission?'

'In a nutshell, old boy. In a nutshell,' agreed Wagstaff-Jones, scooping up the remainder of the pistachios.

6
Mr Pritchard

The phone rang and a quavering voice asked whether it was I who was speaking. I said, 'Speaking,' and waited.

After a pause the caller told me his name was Pritchard and that he had been given my name by the School of Oriental and African Studies as someone who gave lessons in Arabic.

'That was some time ago,' I said, for I was now of the opinion that teaching was one of the less materially rewarding ways of trying to make a living.

'Oh, I was so hoping... I recently read your article about the Arabic short story and I would so have liked...'

As he didn't continue I was forced to fill in the silence, so I asked him at what standard he was.

'Oh, just an enthusiastic amateur's,' he said. 'I can read through a newspaper with a lot of difficulty and the help of a dictionary – I use *Wehr*, I hope you agree it's the best available – but often I find phrases or whole sentences whose meaning eludes me...'

He had the habit of suddenly coming to a stop mid-sentence and leaving one with the weight of a conversation to keep going. Before I realized it I had agreed to a price per hour for two lessons a week, Mondays and Thursdays, to begin the coming Monday. No sooner had I replaced the receiver than I regretted having given in.

When, on Monday at six, Mr Pritchard appeared at the flat door he was even more aged than he had sounded on the telephone. My flat was on the second floor and possessed no lift, and when I answered the bell he had the look about him of someone about to pay for his excessive exertions.

'Pritchard,' he said breathlessly and extended a claw-like hand. 'It's very good of you to agree to give me lessons,' he said almost at once, sinking into an armchair. 'I hope I didn't appear too insistent.'

I mumbled something in reply and sat in the other armchair beside which stood a small table on which I had arranged a pile of Arabic books and a recent newspaper. I looked across at my pupil and guessed him to be in his late seventies or even early eighties. Though tall and well-built, he had an air of great fragility about him, with skin that looked as if it had been too tightly drawn across the space that lay between one bone and the next. I wondered at the effort he had to make to come across London from the hotel on Cromwell Road in which he had told me he lived.

As though reading my thoughts, he said: 'When I journey out from the stronghold of my hotel these days I make use of London's excellent taxi service. It's a small luxury I allow myself – a concession to my advancing years... What a ridiculous phrase that is, "advancing years", as though the years ever retreat!'

We both laughed and I then passed the newspaper to him and asked him to read out loud the passage I had marked; in this way I would quickly be able to determine the extent of his knowledge of the language. I was surprised at the accuracy with which he read, even correctly supplying many of the final vowel sounds. His slurred speech, however, became more apparent when he spoke Arabic and it was difficult for me to follow. Of his own accord he stopped and laid the paper down.

'A year or two ago,' he told me, 'I had a minor stroke and this has rendered the pronunciation of certain Arabic letters even more difficult for me, not that I ever really got my tongue round some of them.'

'You have an unusually good command of the language,' I said, trying not to sound patronizing.

'Oh no, I'm only too aware of the gaps in my knowledge. Anyway, don't the Arabs have an expression about perfection being with Allah alone?'

'That's right,' I said.

'You see, I never had the benefit of really breaking the back of the language at a university. It's too difficult a language to study on one's own as I've been trying to do these past few years. Of course, in the Sudan Political Service – that's where I spent my time – one was required to learn enough to get about; in fact, one had to take a series of examinations before one got one's promotion, but there wasn't much encouragement – or indeed time – to come to grips with the niceties of the classical language.'

He then recounted to me that he once had a clerk called Abduh Ibrahim who was an avid admirer of the poet Abu Nuwas, famed for his verses in praise of wine. Abduh Ibrahim, it seemed, was also in the habit of indulging a liking for liquor and Mr Pritchard had often to turn a blind eye to his arriving at work the worse for wear.

He leaned back in the armchair and, with eyes closed, declaimed in sonorous Arabic Abu Nuwas's most famed line of poetry which, translated, reads: 'Leave off blaming me, for blame is an incitement, but cure me rather with that which was the ailment.'

'Now there's poetry for you!' he commented with enthusiasm, then added: 'I recently tried to read some of this so-called modern poetry. I found it difficult to understand and what I did understand did not impress me greatly.'

I said that I tended to agree with him, then reminded myself that I was the teacher and that the lesson had got out of hand; in fact, it had scarcely begun and the hour was now nearly up. Determined that the next lesson we would start work in earnest, I found out from him that he did not know of the delightful autobiography of the blind Egyptian scholar Taha Hussein and, therefore, informed him that we would read through the first volume together, the volume dealing with his childhood in a village in Upper Egypt. Mr Pritchard was to prepare several pages and we would then go through them during our lesson. I told him that the book could be obtained from one or other of the shops in Great Russell Street.

Though our subsequent progress through Taha Hussein's autobiography was slow, we both, I think, enjoyed the experience. The reading was interspersed with numerous questions from Mr Pritchard about refinements of grammar, the peculiar, attractively hesitant style of the blind scholar, and about details of the great man's later life and other writings. I came to realize that for my pupil the lessons meant more than merely adding to his store of the language: they were important landmarks in his uneventful week.

He was scrupulously correct about not taking up

more than an hour of my time and would always have the exact amount of money in an envelope which he would leave discreetly on the table before rising to go.

Then, one evening after our hour was over, I asked him whether he'd like a coffee, a cup of Turkish coffee. His eyes lit up. 'You have a *kanaka*?'

Yes, I had a *kanaka*.

'And where do you manage to buy the right kind of coffee?'

I told him there were a number of places in Soho and elsewhere.

He sipped at the coffee with delight. 'It takes me back,' he said and a shadow flitted across his worn face. For a moment I thought he was going to reminisce, but he seemed to check himself. Seeing that the coffee was still too hot to drink other than in sips, I asked him whether he remembered the terms for the different degrees of sweetness at which one could ask for one's coffee to be served. It obviously gave him great pleasure to dredge his memory for the various words.

'And for a coffee without any sugar at all?'

He hesitated, then said triumphantly: '*Sada*,' and hauling himself to his feet, apologized for taking up my time and slipped the prepared envelope alongside the coffee cup.

As the lessons continued I would make a point of setting aside the last quarter of an hour for our having coffee together. Sometimes, perhaps because of a linguistic point that had arisen, I would ask him about some aspect of life in Sudan and, almost apologetically, he would recount an anecdote that came to mind. 'One felt, in those days, that one was in the very midst of life,' he commented once, 'not... not...' And for loss of words or in order not to upset himself (or me), he just clasped his large hands in front of him in a gesture that expressed a grim finality.

With time I felt myself being insidiously cast in an ever more important role in his barren life, a role I felt both unwilling and inadequate to perform. At the same time, too, I was conscious of a growing fondness for the old man who, I told myself, besides being several generations my senior, was so utterly unlike me.

We were about halfway through the first volume of Taha Hussein's autobiography when, sipping at his coffee after a lesson, he suddenly said: 'I remember once a Sudanese friend of mine saying to me that if he hadn't been born a Sudanese he'd like to have been an Englishman. He was an exceptional man — someone who, like Taha Hussein, had risen from humble beginnings – and I took it as a great compliment to ourselves. I replied to him in like terms: that if I weren't English I'd have opted for being Sudanese. This was no empty compliment on my part. I meant it... I really liked and admired them immensely. It always seemed to me a pity that the English and they couldn't somehow get closer together after we left.'

He removed some coffee grounds from his mouth with a finger and rubbed them off against the side of the saucer.

'If I'd had any sort of courage – I mean real courage, not just the sort they give medals for – I'd have stayed on in Sudan. After all, that was where my heart was... Instead of being retired and becoming an old fogey ending my days in a hotel on Cromwell Road where it's all bridge and tittle-tattle, I should have left the service and bought myself a few *feddans* of land and a little village house somewhere... I could then have found myself a well-shaped Fatima or Zeinab – and if it meant becoming a Muslim, what's so terrible about that? I can think of a lot worse things to be than a God-fearing Muslim who rises with the dawn to perform his first prayers of the day.'

He gave me a man-to-man look from under his bushy eyebrows. 'No doubt my Fatima would have brought me to an early grave – the Sudanese women are renowned for their voracious sexual appetites – but it's senseless to measure life in terms of years... The sad fact is that one can live too long... one can outlive oneself.'

A surreptitious look at my watch revealed that we were ten minutes beyond our time. I suspected that he had seldom talked with such frankness to anyone and that, having overcome his natural reluctance to talk about himself, he would like to continue. I, in my turn, was being shown another side of the old man and felt that my time was not being wasted by listening to him.

'Hardly the done thing for a member of the Sudan Service?' I suggested.

'Oh, the English would have simply hated it!' he remarked vehemently. 'Poor old Pritchard's gone native,' they'd have said in their various clubs. But what could they have done about it? Nothing. And if that was what I wanted to do with the rest of my life, I should have gone ahead and done it . . . Most of us are far too frightened about what the neighbours might say to do something which is regarded as unconventional. And such cowardice – all cowardice – is paid for dearly.'

He stared dreamily ahead of him for some moments, apparently oblivious of my presence, then pulled himself to his feet and took himself off in search of a taxi.

One day, looking through my bookshelves, I came across two copies of a small Arabic textbook I had compiled and printed in Cairo many years previously.

'I thought you might like to have a copy,' I told him at the end of his next visit and extended the book.

He took it almost reverently. 'Are you sure you can spare it?' He looked at the title page. 'Would you write something in it?'

It hadn't occurred to me that he might make such a request and I was momentarily at a loss as to what to say. Then I borrowed his pen and wrote:

'To Mr Pritchard, in friendship,' and signed it and added the date.

He read what I had written and smiled. 'That's very good of you. I'll treasure it.'

He got up and pumped my hand.

'Till Monday,' I said.

'*Inshallah*,' he answered, as scrupulous as a fervent Muslim in not speaking of anything in the future without adding this phrase.

'*Inshallah*,' I repeated.

But it was not God's will that we should have another lesson. On the Monday, shortly before six, the telephone rang and a genteel voice informed me that it was the manageress of the Kingsley Hotel and that, before being taken to hospital after a heart attack, Sir Hugh Pritchard had asked that she ring me to say he wouldn't be able to continue with his lessons.

'I'm sorry to say that Sir Hugh died in the ambulance on his way to the hospital. The old gentleman will be sadly missed by all the staff here.'

The Times gave him pride of place in the obituary column. After detailing his distinguished career it had ended by mentioning that his wife had died many years previously 'in tragic circumstances' and that his only son had been killed in the North Africa campaign. I suspect, though, that few people attended his funeral. As perhaps his best friend at the time of his death, I should have made the effort.

7

Garbage Girl

From time to time I lifted my eyes from the typewriter and looked down through the bare network of branches that later in the summer would be carrying a scarlet carpet of flame-of-the-forest. A few feet above the towering blocks of flats that stood along the banks of the Nile hung a biscuit-coloured layer of pollution: a huge dome that acted like a mute to the sun's rays. Each time, when there was no sign of her, I returned to my work, but my mind was only half on it. It was the time of day, mid-morning, when she and her young brother and the donkey cart would appear, though sometimes they would miss a day – not necessarily a Muslim Friday or a Christian Sunday. Then, suddenly, there was the sound of the bell. I jumped

to my feet and there, four floors below, stood the
rickety cart with its two sore-ridden donkeys. They
were near the end of their round and the cart was
almost filled with garbage. It was ringed with
balancing cats who fought among themselves as
they gingerly dipped their paws into the muck and
sometimes succeeded in clawing up something to
eat. I could see her young brother, his basket slung
over his shoulder and almost scraping the ground,
making his way from the large villa opposite and
leaving behind him a trail of lettuce leaves and balls
of soiled cotton wool.

She stood at the door, her half-filled basket at her
feet. The dirty kerchief round her head I recognized
as the piece of batik I'd once bought in Bangkok and
passed on to her. With her pouty mouth she smiled
at me. She was twelve maybe, maybe even less, but
in Western terms no longer a child. Her large,
beautifully shaped eyes demanded that she be
thought of as a woman, a woman who was somehow
able to appear detached from the reeking filth with
which she worked. She was tall and thin and had a
way of carrying herself that emphasized the nipples·
of two recently sprouted breasts straining against the
stained *gallabia*. Underneath it she was as naked as
when her mother had brought her into the light, for
once she had bent down and collected a couple of
eggshells that had bounced off the edge of her
basket, and the image of her light brown thighs and
buttocks had stayed in my mind.

'*Shouf rigli*,' I heard her say and I brought my eyes down from her breasts to her feet. She lifted one foot and I saw that it had a piece of dirty rag around it. 'A bit of glass wounded me,' she explained, dragging the rag aside so I could see the deep gash in her instep.

I told her to be careful about it, that I didn't have anything for it but that she should get some antiseptic. I turned away from her and searched in my pocket for a pound. 'Go to the chemist's beyond the *maidan*,' I told her, 'and he'll give you something for it.'

'It was a bit of glass,' she said to me again, taking the note from me. I then remembered that I'd saved some sweets for her, so I went back into the living-room and brought them to her. She pocketed them without enthusiasm; she knew what they were: the sweets that Cairo's groceries gave instead of small change now that piastre pieces had, with inflation, become worth more in pure metal than their face value. Some of Cairo's recent hard-faced millionaires who drove around in white Mercedes were making the money for their silk shirts and pointed Italian shoes from melting down these old coins. The grocers gave you small change in book of matches or sweets, and since knowing Suha I'd been taking my change in sweets.

'Be careful about your foot,' I told her again. 'You should wear shoes,' I added.

She gave me a look which said: I'll wear shoes

when someone like you cares to give me a pair.

'One day, God willing, I'll give you some money for a pair of shoes.'

'Don't you have an old pair?' she asked. 'A pair you don't want?'

'They'd be too big for you,' I said.

'Better than too small,' she said with a laugh.

I remembered the pair of canvas shoes that were giving at the toes. They'd be double her size but she could slop around in them and they'd be some protection. I took them out from the bottom of the cupboard in the bedroom and handed them to her.

She examined them and put a finger through the hole in one of the toes as though to point out that in no way did they let me out of my promise to give her money for a new pair.

'Thanks,' she said and put them on top of my garbage.

'You're passing by tomorrow?'

'God willing,' she said. The smile she gave me seemed to suck me deep into her eye-sockets.

'God willing,' I said and shut the door on her.

I stood on the balcony and watched her empty my garbage and that of my neighbours into the cart. As it moved down the street and turned into the *maidan*, the cats, finding themselves in foreign territory, jumped down. I returned to the typewriter and tried to continue with the piece I had a deadline on. Instead, I read through the last sentence, then sat back and lit a cigarette and thought that some day I should do a feature about Cairo's garbage people and the hundreds of donkey-drawn carts that collected it up and dumped it alongside the shanty town on the outskirts of the city. For years the government had been thinking of introducing modern refuse lorries and getting the garbage recycled as happened in every other self-respecting capital, but the figures never worked out right. How could you ever compete with the tribe of men and children who collected the city's waste in return for a minimal tip from the householder? They drove their carts in from the Mokattam Hills and their squalid shacks built around the heaps of rubbish. If, going out to the airport, you asked the taxi to take you by the Salah Salem route, past the Citadel and the Mohammed Ali Mosque, you could see the diminutive, overworked donkeys toiling up the steep slope before turning off to the Mokattam Hills. There the garbage people sorted through Cairo's refuse and fed part of it to the pigs they bred; it was said they were all Christians – Copts – for no Muslim would go anywhere near a pig, dead or alive. It was also said that only someone who didn't know the conditions in which the pigs were kept and what they were fed on would ever think of eating pork in Cairo. The garbage people excited sympathy from the foreign community, and the other day there was an item in the English paper about the ambassador's wife paying them a visit and that there was a sort of Mother Teresa who was devoting her life to them. All my Muslim friends said they didn't deserve any help and that they did very well from the strange monopoly they exercised. Perhaps there was a story there, perhaps one day I'd drive out to the Mokattam Hills and see for myself. Perhaps I could an arrange a visit to Suha and her family there.

Can a man, a hard-bitten journalist, in what is euphemistically called middle age, be in love with a refuse-collector of twelve? Can you really call it love? Many would call the emotion unnatural, a perversion, but they would be wrong. Maybe, though, it shouldn't be called love, for it's a sentiment more disturbing than that, a sentiment that hasn't as yet been given a name. Perhaps only certain people are prone to this special love/lust feeling. A man may live with a woman all the years of his life, he may have affair after affair, and yet never know this desperate pain that joins the heart to the crotch. To those who *are* prone to this bane, how often can it occur in a lifetime? To me it had happened three times before: once with the wife of my father's boss when I was fourteen and she approaching her menopause; then, more recently, with a Turkish Cypriot peasant woman who used to make *halloumi* cheese and had a shepherd husband who had done time in prison for knifing someone who'd made a pass at her. Then there was that woman who, sitting opposite with a teenage boy, had shared a carriage on the Underground with me between Russell Square and Green Park and had then stood on the platform and had held my eyes without risk till the train had disappeared on its way to Hyde Park Corner. And now there was Suha, the child with budding breasts and unfledged thighs and a basketful of filth hung round her neck, who daily rang the bell.

This unnamed emotion feeds and waxes fat on an exclusive diet of daydreams. As there is an unadmitted acceptance deep, deep down that where this emotion is at play fulfilment cannot be achieved, these daydreams are taken up to and beyond the borders of credulity. Thus, ever since first setting eyes on Suha, I had rehearsed in my mind any number of possible and impossible situations between us: her taking a quick shower before joining me in bed, while her brother waited downstairs and wondered which flat she'd disappeared into; of her somehow escaping from her rounds and making her way secretly back to my flat for an hour, a night, a week. I even saw myself taking her in a taxi to the airport and catching the once-a-week Air France flight to Nice, having her dressed by the boutiques of the Riviera and walking with her along the Promenade des Anglais. The daydreams of self-fulfilment were never-ending but so, too, were the *daymares* (have I coined a word?) of jealousy. Were there not others in whose hearts, as she made her rounds, she had awakened the same feelings, and had not some of them, bolder than me, won from her unthinkable favours?

I abruptly cut off the image of Suha standing naked under the needlepoints of water and forced myself back into the piece my paper had asked for about why Egypt's agriculture was all to hell since Nasser chased out the big landowners and built the Aswan Dam.

Two days passed without anyone turning up for the garbage. It had suddenly become warmer and the pong in the kitchen had begun to build up. Then, on the third day, there was a ring at the door and when I looked down into the street, the cart and the two donkeys were there, also her brother throwing stones at the scavenging cats. But at the door I was faced with someone I'd never seen before: a small man with a wall-eye. Though he looked too young, he told me he was Suha's father, that she was ill at home and that she'd been to the doctor who had said she needed her foot lanced but that he wanted five pounds for doing it. He said all this as though he'd learnt it by heart.

'I'm sorry to hear about your daughter,' I told him and fished in my pocket and gave him a pound note.

'And the rest?' he said, cocking his good eye at the note. 'Where will I get the rest from?'

I thought quickly, then took the pound from his hand and went to the bedroom and searched in my coat pocket. I returned with a five-pound note and handed it to him. He looked surprised rather than grateful.

'May God grant you a long life,' he said.

'May God cure your daughter,' I said and brought him my garbage from the kitchen, then went back to my typewriter. I had sent off my piece on Egypt's agriculture and was now trying to write a final paragraph to my latest story, already overdue, about the political clout of the Muslim fundamentalists.

A week went by and the cart looked after by Suha and her brother was replaced by another one in the charge of two rough-looking, rough-speaking boys who looked like twins. I asked them about Suha but they said they'd never heard of her; I mentioned a young girl who'd cut her foot and they didn't know anything about her either. One of them took fifty piastres from me and came regular as clockwork daily at eleven; their donkeys were larger and better fed and had leather traces instead of the wire ones that bit into the flesh of Suha's skinny couple.

Then the man who said he was Suha's father called round again. He didn't try to deaden the blow but said straight out that Suha had died, that her foot had swollen more and more and that it had got gangrene, and she'd died. Now he wanted money for her burial. I gave him two pounds and shut the door on him. The rest of the morning I spent staring ahead of me into the branches of the flame-of-the-forest tree and wondering whether the garbage people used coffins.

It must have been two months later, it was high summer and the price of Teymour mangoes had come down to as low as they'd be. I was walking through Maidan al-Misaha weighed down with two string-bags of groceries. Shouts and a cloud of dust ahead indicated that a game of football was going on in the road that separated the two plots of coarse grass and sparse flowerbeds. As I jumped ungainly to one side to escape the ball I was sure had been aimed at me, I saw her sitting beyond one of the heaps of clothes that indicated a goalpost. Stately as Cleopatra in her barge, Suha was sitting on the cart with her feet resting on the front nearside wheel. She was puffing at a cigarette and the smoke curled up in the still air forming a bluish-grey plume to the red kerchief round her head. Though her gaze was directed towards me she made no sign of having seen me. My heart began to beat heavily and I became conscious of the strings of the bags cutting into my palms. I braced my shoulders and tried to stride on as though oblivious of her presence, but as I reached the turning to my street I felt the strength go out of my legs. As though a great lump of cat's fur had lodged itself in my chest, I suddenly found difficulty in breathing. I had a moment's fear that this was how one felt when about to have a heart attack. I came to a stop and rested the heavy bags on the ground. I glanced back at her and saw that she was looking in my direction. Her tall, upright figure was posed against the darkening sky; her hand with the cigarette was resting against her cheek. I took up the bags and walked forward several steps. When I looked round again she was blocked out by the new apartment building that was going up on the corner of the *maidan*. With a deep sadness, a nostalgia that was well familiar to me, I knew I'd never see her again.

8
Coffee at the Marriott

Eva and Amanda had nothing very much in common except that they were both English and had married Egyptians. The husbands, too, had little in common: Galal Hafiz, a Muslim, was a professor of medieval Egyptian history at one of the several government universities in Cairo, while Ramses Nada was a Copt who ran a successful tourist business mainly with Germany and Italy. The former was of course ill-paid, but scraped together extra money over and above his meagre salary by writing books and articles and serving on various committees, while his wife taught at one of the English-language schools that were of recent vogue; in fact her salary almost matched that of her husband. Ramses Nada, on the other hand, with diverse interests in the tourism field, had become one of Cairo's fat cats, with a large 757 BMW which he was accustomed to drive while talking into his mobile telephone.

Eva and her husband lived in a modest flat on the less prosperous side of Garden City; they led an existence free of financial worries but one that allowed for few luxuries. Once a year she bought herself a return ticket to the UK and would spend six weeks with her sister in Chichester on the south coast. Once every four years Galal would accompany her and they would treat themselves to a week in London, staying at the same boarding house in Earls Court where she had at first consented to spend a night with him when they were both students. Having learnt, since living in Egypt, of the high value placed on a hymen that was intact, especially among conservative Muslim families such as Galal's, she had always had a feeling of deep gratitude and admiration towards him for marrying her after that night of illicit love. Despite her initial difficulties of settling into an alien culture, the two enjoyed a happy marriage; this, too, despite the fact that she had given him but a single child, a daughter who had died with shattering suddenness at the age of twelve.

Amanda, on the other hand, lived just across from the Marriott Hotel in Zamalek, in a luxurious penthouse. She, too, once she had come to terms with the fact that her husband, in spite of his many good qualities – which included a genuine love of her and their children – was a congenital womanizer, led a full and contented life. The two English women, so different in their circumstances and background, had over the years become fast friends.

For the past several years the two women talked most days on the phone and met up on Tuesdays for coffee and cakes at the Marriott. At first their conversation revolved round their personal histories and how they had come to marry Egyptians and to make Cairo their home. Then, with time, their conversation came to focus on their daily lives: Eva's work at the school, Galal's squabbles with his colleagues, Amanda's bridge parties and the misbehaviour of her two children (one of each) who were now students at the American University and her fears that the girl would lose her virginity and the boy would get into drugs.

Today Amanda arrived first and chose a corner table. She immediately noticed, as her friend came towards her, that Eva's face wore an unusually solemn expression. They kissed and Amanda enquired if anything was wrong. Eva shook her head and suggested they choose their cakes first. As they stood at the counter looking down at the display of cakes, Amanda was surprised to find her friend saying, 'I think I'll have a chocolate one today.' Normally she would choose the least fattening on show.

As they forked up the first mouthful of cake, Eva announced in a low voice and with a twisted smile on her face, 'I have just discovered that Galal had another wife.'

Amanda was taken aback but finished her mouthful before querying, 'You mean he divorced her?'

'No, it seems she died,' answered Eva.

'Was he already married when he married you?' her friend enquired.' 'After all, he's a Muslim and he's entitled to have four wives if it comes to it.'

'Oh, I know all that,' said Eva with a certain impatience in her voice, 'but I think he could at least have told me.'

They sipped at their coffees and picked at their cakes for some minutes in silence before Amanda asked: 'So he didn't tell you?'

Eva shook her head.

'Do you mind very much?'

Eva dabbed at her eyes with a paper handkerchief that she had taken from her bag. 'Yes, I think I do, but I don't see there's anything I can do about it.'

'And how did you find out?'

Eva looked embarrassed as she explained that while tidying Galal's papers in his study she had come across an envelope addressed to herself in English in his handwriting and marked 'To be opened at my death'. 'I steamed it open,' she confessed, 'and was rewarded for my dishonesty with the information that, before being sent to

England to do his doctorate, he had married his cousin. The letter stated that the woman is no longer alive but he has a grown-up son by her who still lives in his village outside Minya. I suspect that every now and again, when he tells me he's been invited away to give a lecture, he is in fact visiting his son. After all, I suppose it's only natural . . .'

Amanda broke the silence that followed by rising to her feet. 'Perhaps we should each have another cake,' she suggested. 'Today's on me.'

When they were seated once again with fresh plates and cakes and had ordered two more *cappuccinos*, Eva informed her friend in a calmer voice: 'If I'm honest with myself and don't get all emotional about it, I suppose I'm pleased for his sake that he has a son. As you know, after Dina died I wasn't able to give him more children. I would naturally have been upset if he'd taken another wife at that time. After all, Dina's death was something we suffered together, and it would somehow have been disrespectful to her memory, besides being hurtful to me. What he did before he and I met is really neither here nor there. Is it?' She appealed to Eva for reassurance.

'No, it's not,' answered Amanda who, as a result of her own life, had become unusually broadminded in such matters. 'It's just how you look at things.' She then asked whether the letter contained anything else.

Having blown her nose, Eva looked across at her

friend with a bright smile. 'The letter gave several details about money and what I should do in the event of his death. In the last sentence he said that he had never loved anyone else in his life.'

'That was nice,' commented Amanda.

Eva nodded her head but had the look of someone whose tears would flow if she attempted to say anything at that moment.

'And what did you do with the letter?'

'I got some glue and sealed it up again and then I put it back among his papers,' Eva said simply. 'The only thing I regret, though, is that I ever opened it in the first place.'

9

The Garden of Sheikh Osman

The three donkeys came to a stop outside the double gate with the iron bosses. It was early afternoon and the parallel shadows of the donkeys and their riders pointed at an angle towards the high mud wall that enclosed the garden of date-palms that had the Nile as one of its other boundaries.

The middle figure, a tall thin boy named Jaafar, was dressed in a starched *gallabia* of a blinding whiteness and a vast matching turban that seemed to balance uneasily on his finely featured ebony face. He clapped his hands and called out. He turned to his younger companion, a white boy who rode on his right, and they exchanged a few words. As bolts were drawn back and the wings of the gate were dragged open, the two boys, jostling for position, raced through the opening. The white boy, who was the first to enter the shaded world of the garden, wore khaki shorts and a khaki jacket with bulging pockets; his head was protected against the intense heat of the Sudanese summer by a wide-brimmed, double-felted hat. The third member of the trio, by name Shakir, was the white boy's servant; he was dressed in a faded blue *gallabia* and a knitted skullcap and was barefoot. His face was creased into a worried frown, brought on no doubt by the responsibilities of looking after the welfare and safety of the son of the local district commissioner.

'I won!' called out the white boy whose real name was David and whom Jaafar called Daoud.

'It's your donkey that won,' Jaafar corrected him. 'That donkey of yours is more like a horse – and the three boys broke into guffaws of laughter.

The date garden that lay between the Nile and the surrounding desert was just over a mile from the sprawling township in which its owner, Sheikh Osman Abdul Gader, had his shop. The township's leading silversmith, he was descended from one of the great families of Kordofan, while his wife Fatima, whose last child Jaafar was, came from one of the cattle-rearing Kababeesh and had brought considerable wealth and connections with her. Such tourists as visited the township, having come down from the Egyptian border by steamboat, seldom left without having bought some momento from Sheikh Osman's shop, be it merely a silver ashtray with an old coin from the Mahdi's time in the centre. Though a stranger might think he was just the owner of a shop that sold things made of silver and had a meagre selection of watches, Sheikh Osman was in fact one of the most substantial merchants in the area. He was engaged in the lucrative trade of taking cattle and camels on the hoof into Egypt, often as far north as Cairo itself; he also bought up much of the date crop of the district for sale to Khartoum's traders. In addition, rumour had it that he traded in the illegal sale of Pharaonic relics rifled from tombs higher up the river. All in all, he was a man to be reckoned with and he was happy to see that his son Jaafar had become a good friend of the young son of the district commissioner; if nothing else, it gave him extra kudos.

The contrast in temperature between outside the date-garden and inside was extreme. It even brought a momentary shiver to the riders as they trotted along the mud pathways that ran beside runnels of fast-flowing water sprinkled with flickering coins of sunlight. Delicate rust-coloured doves moved in the branches of the lofty date-palms, making their soft soporific calls. To the English boy it seemed a place without horizons, where there were always new corners to be explored, more water courses to be followed and more bewhiskered and blindfolded water-buffaloes to watch as they walked tirelessly round and round the creaking water-wheels. It was a world of magic and his friend Jaafar held the key to it.

By one of the *sagias*, or water-wheels, that was no longer worked, the three boys dismounted. Shakir, having swept a patch of ground with a dried palm frond, spread out a blanket. The English boy produced six small hard-boiled eggs wrapped up in a handkerchief, also a tin of peaches in syrup and an opener, while Jaafar untied a small bundle and revealed several *koftas* that his mother had made and some rounds of bread. After they had eaten and Shakir was washing the metal plates, the English boy divided up the toffees he had brought between Jaafar and himself, but Jaafar insisted that Shakir should share equally with them and the English boy reluctantly agreed. Then Jaafar got up to rinse his hands in the running water that passed close by and the English boy saw him scooping water into his mouth and spitting it out again, so he imitated him. After that the two boys walked to a flat area behind the *sagia* where they had laid out in the sun the mud figures they had made the last time they had picnicked in the garden.

There were figures of donkeys and camels, also miniature water-pitchers and cooking pots. There were also two human figures, to one of which the English boy had, as an afterthought, attached an outsize penis. Jaafar, however, had objected and the

English boy could see where his Sudanese friend had insisted on pinching off the offending protuberance. The other figure had breasts of different sizes. When the English boy had asked what a woman had 'down there', Jaafar feigned ignorance.

'Nothing,' he had said.

'How does she pee?'

'She has a hole,' Jaafar conceded and the two boys laughed at the idea.

The English boy destroyed the various figures by kicking at them. 'We'll make some more next time,' he told Jaafar.

They said goodbye and arranged to meet the following day in the souk. Then the English boy and his servant rode off towards the row of bungalows that stood directly on the bank of the Nile, while Jaafar went back to the straggling family home that housed his father's shop.

The English boy had his bath and was sitting in his dressing-gown having his supper. His mother was sitting beside him and reading out loud. Each time she turned a page, she would show him the picture alongside the text. The boy had had the book read to him several times and knew it almost by heart. He therefore paid little attention to his mother, though he enjoyed having her there while he ate. Then his father came in with a serious look on his face and didn't say anything, only indicated to his mother that she should leave the room with him.

'David,' she said to him when she returned, 'something's happened to Jaafar.' She went over to him and began hugging and kissing him. She told him that there'd been some accident with a hurricane lamp and that Jaafar's clothing had caught fire.

'Can I go and see him?' asked the boy.

She shook her head and said that Jaafar was dead. The boy was at a loss as to how to react to the news. When he saw that her eyes were watering, he burst out crying.

She calmed him down and put him to bed and she was relieved when he slept right away after his full day. The next morning he asked about Jaafar and his mother told him that, if he liked, he could go and see Sheikh Osman and tell him how sorry he was about Jaafar.

'He'll be at his house,' she told him, and he set off with Shakir. When he arrived at Sheikh Osman's house, he felt nervous and wished he hadn't come. He dismounted and looked across at the large reception room where he saw Jaafar's father receiving condolences from the leading men of the town. He thought of going away again, but a servant came out and led him to a smaller reception room. He stood there for a few minutes looking at the gilt chairs ranged round the room before Jaafar's father entered. The old man greeted him and held his hand in both of his; the boy knew that there was something he should be saying to

Sheikh Osman. If only Jaafar were there; he could have asked him.

'Can I see him?' he asked awkwardly.

The old man sat down and put his arm round the boy.

'He was buried yesterday evening,' explained Sheikh Osman and the boy could feel the old man's tears being caught in his sparse white beard and their wetness against his cheek. It was the first time he had seen a grown-up cry. The boy remembered the time, some weeks back, when his cat had been bitten by a scorpion and he'd found its body lying on the veranda. He and his mother had put it in a shoe-box and had buried it in the garden.

He thought about Jaafar and what it meant to be buried in the ground, and he thought too about never going again to the garden of Sheikh Osman.

10
Cat

He woke to the feel of the dead weight of Cat against his drawn-up legs. His head was heavy with the sleep of old age but, as he did every morning, he told himself that the cat must be fed. Rising, he searched with his feet for his slippers. Cat, knowing that her companion would be away some time in the bathroom before appearing for breakfast, sidled out through the half-open bedroom window and tripped down the flight of steps to the terrace. There she curled up and went to sleep on the rush matting with its zebra stripes from the trellis roofing of evenly placed palm fronds.

The old man prepared their two breakfasts: warmed milk with bits of bread soaked in it for Cat and for himself several cups of weak tea and a round of the local bread, crisped on an iron grid over the gas ring, with white cheese and honey. When Cat had finished her milk he fed her some of the white cheese.

He turned on the radio to the World Service of the BBC. It struck him – not for the first time – that had a news bulletin from ten years back been substituted for today's it would not have sounded out of place. On the other hand, listening morning and evening to the news had become part of the routine of his life. With age, his life had become more and more one of routine, one in most of which Cat participated.

While it was still cool enough he walked out into the courtyard garden of dark red, white and tile-coloured bougainvillaea that clung to the surrounding mud walls and mingled with the heavily scented jasmine. Hibiscus bushes flouted their scarlet flowers and pots of various sorts of cacti showed his particular fondness for these austere plants. Cat followed at his heels. Every now and again he bent down and passed his hand over the head and down the leopard-streaked body.

He passed through the courtyard into the open garden and was faced by a full view of the expanse of dark blue lake, with beyond the sand-dune hills that reflected the shadows of passing clouds. The hills were in turn reflected in the unruffled waters that divided them from the tiny village perched on an outcrop of rock, with bright green fields of clover and the occasional tightly barbered date-palm. Today a man was ploughing with two oxen and the dark brown carpet of earth was dotted with white egrets in search of food in the ploughed troughs.

He walked down the sloping patch of land, examining as he went several straggly fig trees already showing fruit but from which the birds were more likely to profit than he. He continued on to the lower boundary of his *feddan* of land where he had had a simple cement seat made under the shade of an old sant tree that had been there even before he bought the land and built the house. He sat for some time, with Cat circling round his legs, counting off in his mind the houses that stretched to either side of him along the ridge of rock on which the village had grown. Mostly they were traditional mud houses in which the original peasants still lived, while others, some built of stone with domes in imitation of the style made popular by the architect Hasan Fathi, belonged to families from the capital. Most, though, were visited less and less by their owners as 'the simple life' became increasingly less attractive and could be led with greater panache along the shores of the Red Sea or the tourist villages of Sinai.

The time had passed when he hoped that someone from the capital might decide to drive out and visit him. He was now so divorced from what concerned most people that he was aware of having nothing to say to fill the gaps of silence that punctuated his meetings with those who had been friends and with whom he had once upon a time shared interests. He was conscious that where most people were concerned he had become a bore: he could see people's attention wandering as he talked of village matters or of Cat's latest antics.

The call to morning prayers interrupted his reverie and informed him that he should make his way back to the house to prepare his midday meal. Yesterday the old fisherman with his donkey had called and he had bought some of the small sole which were plentiful in the lake at this time of the year. Having steamed them, he fed himself and Cat, then retired to his bedroom for his afternoon nap, taking with him a paperback novel which he had been trying to finish for the past week. Cat joined him in the bedroom but left directly after her master's head had fallen sideways on the pillow and the book had slipped from his grasp.

Two hours later he went down again to the living-room and turned on the television. He was surprised to find no Cat awaiting him but judged that some hunting expedition had perhaps taken her further afield than usual. He kept the sound on the television down as he watched a scene of young Palestinian boys pelting long-legged Teutonic-looking Israelis with stones. Then he heard the kitchen door being opened and closed. Perhaps Hasan was bringing him the eggs he had asked for.

He looked round and saw his tall neighbour in baggy white trousers holding up a cat by the neck. He was about to protest when he realized that the animal was dead and that it was Cat. Hasan wished him a good evening and moved forward and placed the dead cat on the rush mat, then turned and explained that he had found the body lying by the old chicken-house. He gave it as his opinion that Cat had been bitten by a scorpion.

The old man rose to his feet and crouched down by the cat. When he touched the body there was a complete absence of life about it; her pink tongue peeped out from between lips set in a rictus smile. He let her head drop back to the mat and his eyes travelled down to the swollen belly with its dead kittens. He wondered how long there had been still to go before she would have given birth.

As though reading his thoughts, Hasan said: 'You could have taken one of her children.'

'Yes,' he said, thinking it strange that death should not have spared her the few days necessary for her to deliver her new batch of kittens. It would have made such a difference to him.

'Shall I throw her away?' asked Hasan.

He was momentarily hurt by the question but for Hasan a dead cat was nothing but refuse.

'Leave her there,' he said.

Hasan hesitated, then wished him good-night and left.

He locked the door behind Hasan and returned

to where the cat lay. As though to underline for him the reality of death a procession of small ants was already moving in the direction of the body.

He went to the kitchen and took out a clean red–and–white check drying–up cloth and wrapped the stiffening body in it. From the shed that led off the kitchen, and which had contained a decrepit car in the days when he could still drive, he took up a hoe and dragged it slowly behind him as he walked into the garden.

The day's heat still lay between the evenly spaced olive trees which had recently had their fortnightly watering. He chose a place close to the boundary wall and with difficulty dug a small grave. He stood for a while, breathless, resting on the handle of the hoe.

He told himself that Hasan would have done it in a tenth of the time, but it was something that he owed Cat. He laid her in the hole, wrapped carefully in the cloth, then filled it with earth and searched round for three stones to place on top.

There came to his mind an image more than seventy years old of a small boy being helped by his mother to lay out his dead cat in a shoe-box and bury it.

Tomorrow he would tell Hasan where he had buried Cat and would ask him not to disturb the mound.

Back in the house he sat in front of the TV screen. He felt emptied, as though the final tenuous thread with life had snapped. In the morning Hasan would surely suggest bringing him another cat, just as he had brought him Cat. He decided it would be pointless — if it had been meant, enough time would have been granted to Cat to deliver her kittens.

11
A Short Weekend

Among the people standing behind the rails that separated those just coming off planes from those awaiting them was the man I guessed to be Roberto. This was confirmed when I saw the piece of cardboard he was holding against his chest and on which my name had been written in a mixture of capital and lower-case letters: MattHeWS. I acknowledged my identity by waving at him as I passed on my way to retrieve my bag and see it through customs. I was surprised to note that several people who had been on the plane with me had already met up with friends and relatives and were moving off towards the line of taxis and the car park. I was astonished to find this laxness among a people whom I thought of as sticklers for doing things right. I felt that this would provide a topic for small-talk with Roberto on the drive. In the event, I forgot to mention it to him.

My bag, just too big to go as cabin luggage, was given only a cursory glance by the customs men and was immediately taken from me by Roberto. He had got himself a trolley, but rightly considering the bag too light to require one, he returned it to the long line of others and regained his ten-franc piece.

The car that awaited us in the car park was a hallmark of the people I was spending the weekend with: an open two-seater white 780 Mercedes. There was thus no question of my having to make my mind up about whether to treat Roberto as a chauffeur and sit in the back.

Roberto was more suitably clothed than I for the sun that beat down. He wore dark-blue linen slacks, white plimsolls and a white shirt with a blue collar and blue edgings to the pockets. All I could do, before getting into the car, was strip off my tie and put it with my jacket and suitcase in the boot.

'It will become cooler as we get higher,' Roberto assured me.

He drove the car easily and at speed through the traffic, showing no impatience when his way was blocked by incompetent or selfish drivers. While he talked he continued to keep his eyes on the traffic ahead with frequent glances in the driving mirrors. He enquired of me what sort of weather we had been having in England, giving no indication that he wasn't a friend of the family who had volunteered to pick me up at the airport, except for the initial 'Let me take your case, sir' and his habit of interspersing my name in whatever remarks he made. He informed me that though they had had a very poor start to the summer, it was now sunny and hot during the day and evenings were made cool by a pleasant breeze. Though he spoke with a marked foreign accent, his English was that of someone used to everyday conversations with native speakers. He was certainly an attractive person and I was surprised that Margot's husband had thought to employ him. I presumed he was Italian.

It was as if I had spoken the thought aloud, for he immediately said, 'I am from across the border but have been working for Mr and Mrs Didcot for the last five years. Yes, Mr Matthews, I started working for the gentleman the year before he became ill.'

The car climbed effortlessly into mountains studded with whitewashed villas splashed with stains of bougainvillaea. Spacious lawns of bright green still sprouted the occasional gnarled olive tree from times when these hillsides were farmed by Provençal peasants.

'Mr Matthews — up there is St Paul de Vence,' Roberto said, pointing towards a cluster of picturesque buildings in a setting of grey stone. 'Tourrettes is another twenty minutes from here.'

For the rest of the journey Roberto left me to my thoughts. I needed the time to prepare myself for what, at best, was likely to be a difficult weekend. It was now Saturday and I had only had the phone call on Wednesday evening. Graham, Margot had told me, had expressed a desire to see me. Could I fly into Nice for the weekend? A ticket would of course be sent to me and I would be picked up at the airport. Then and there I had had to make up my mind. It wasn't easy, especially as I found it unlikely that Graham had in fact requested my presence. It was nine or ten years since I had last heard her voice, the voice of the woman who had for a short and turbulent period been my wife. Of course I had known that Graham Didcot, the man for whom I had worked for some years and who had made a fortune out of plastic piping, that man with the razor-sharp mind and a ruthlessness that was even directed against himself, had some time ago begun his journey towards second childhood. I had merely stored the information away with little feeling one way or the other, and had tried to get on with my own somewhat unsatisfactory life. The fact is that when one's wife starts an affair with the person who is both a friend and one's boss, and they announce to you – as to someone who is scarcely involved – that they intend to marry, one's world is turned upside down. To have to start life anew in one's fifties is to be made to face oneself with a vengeance. I had somehow done so, though without any enthusiasm or success. I had neither Graham's capacity for hard work and his ability to collect round himself people who could further his interests, nor his dogged determination. 'The trouble with you, Jack,' I remember his once saying to me, 'is that you don't really get your teeth into things.' Though I found it wounding, it was not meant to be so – Graham was at heart a kindly man. I suppose I was lucky to get something of a golden handshake out of it, though I inevitably had the feeling that it was more for not putting obstacles in the way of a divorce than for any services I had rendered his company. Business, I must admit, never appealed to me and I would never have wound up in it had it not been for my somewhat unlikely friendship with Graham, based in large part on a shared interest in the game of bridge. When that friendship came to an untimely end, I could hardly expect to stay on with his company.

During my years of marriage to Margot I often told myself – and occasionally her – that were it not for the necessity of earning a living that would keep us in genteel comfort, I would have preferred to pursue a career of letters. Once I was divorced, I was free to do just that. Perhaps, though, the chance had come too late, for the two novels I had written since that date lacked the vibrancy of the sole one that had achieved publication. With my divorce my life had become one of loneliness and of a lower standard of living than I had enjoyed when employed by Graham. At the back of my mind during the days of marriage had also been the thought that, if free again, I would realize those sexual dreams which all but the happiest husbands entertain. But even there things did not turn out as I had hoped and soon old age was looming rather bleakly, for it was only when I lost Margot that I realized what a large piece she represented in the jigsaw of my life.

I had worked it out on the journey up, that Margot would now be fifty: six years my junior and twelve years younger than Graham. This meant that poor Graham, for all his razor-sharp mind, had begun his descent into senility at a relatively early age.

We arrived at the *mas* of the Didcots, signposted as 'Les Hirondelles', some twenty minutes after passing St Paul. It had been bought, I was told, with the money he made out of the deal in buses with the Iranian government that Graham had somehow rowed himself into; nothing to do with plastic piping. It had been while I was still working for him. I had, on his behalf, paid a couple of visits to Teheran and had been responsible for making the arrangements by which a certain local general of considerable clout with the municipality was to receive a healthy cut on the deal. I myself gained little for my part in the affair except for Graham's thanks and several evenings laced with vodka and the best caviare in the world in the company of the general at Shemran's most expensive restaurants. Graham, for all his bonhomie and extravagant ways, was not a particularly generous man.

Lying on the outskirts of the village of Tourrettes, the *mas* had grounds extending over a couple of hectares. The views were fabulous and included glimpses of the sea. The tree-lined drive allowed no sighting of the main elegant stone building until the car drew up in front of it. Margot came out to greet me as Roberto removed my case and coat from the boot.

No doubt the kind sunshine of France's Riviera, the casually good clothes and the easy life she led all contributed to her air of well-being. I told her that she looked splendidly well and I meant it. She presented a tanned cheek for kissing and immediately told me how well *I* looked, which I knew to be a lie, and an unnecessary one at that; I could not have looked particularly well as I did not feel it and didn't live the sort of life that would allow me to look other than older than my age. A mere eight years ago, I reminded myself, this woman had been my wife.

'One is never sure with planes,' she explained, 'so we went ahead and had our lunch without you. I've put Graham to bed for his afternoon siesta. I know what miserable meals they give you on those planes, so I'm having a plate of cold salmon and salad taken to your room. I suggest you have a rest after your journey and we can all meet for drinks beside the pool around six.'

A maid led me to a bedroom with a bathroom leading off it; both were air-conditioned. I had a shower and on returning to the bedroom found that the promised meal, together with what was obviously a home-made strawberry mousse, stood on the central table; a bottle of Sancerre – it was not lost on me that it was the wine that she and I had indulged in as and when my fortunes had permitted – rested in an ice-bucket. As it had already been opened, I poured myself a glass, which I sipped as I drew back the curtains of the room and watched a gardener setting up sprinklers on the lawn. Then I sat down to the salmon and poured myself another glass and thought about the rest of today and tomorrow. The weekend promised to be interesting: certainly, if Graham hadn't lost his appetite for the good things, the food and wine would be of the best. It was also tantalizing to be once again in close proximity to Margot. Why had I been invited for this weekend when countless weekends had passed since she and I had divorced and she had married again without any such invitation being extended?

I poured myself a third glass. I found it didn't go with the mousse but nevertheless finished it. Then I turned off the air-conditioning, undressed and got in naked between the cool sheets.

I slept heavily and woke with a bad mouth. I

looked at the time and saw that I had slept for more than two hours and that I only just had time to dress and make the six o'clock appointment by the pool.

The two of them were alone by the pool. Graham was sitting in an upright canvas chair under the shade of a parasol mounted in a block of cement; he was wearing white linen trousers and a flowered T-shirt and sandals. She got up as I approached and led me towards Graham who looked up only when she placed her hand on his shoulder.

'It's Jack, dear,' she said to him. 'He's come all the way from London to see you.'

His face was longer and thinner and there was a slackness about the jaw that betrayed the illness that had attacked his brain cells. The only expression in the glance he directed at me was one of hostile suspicion.

'You remember your old friend Jack?' she asked.

'Oh yes,' he said with difficulty and he took his right hand from the arm of the chair and held it towards me. There was no grip to the handshake and it was obvious that he didn't recognize me. He had immediately turned away. She indicated that I should bring up a chair and seat myself on the other side of him. 'What will you drink?' she asked. 'We're both on gin and tonic.'

'That will do fine.'

'Ice and lemon?'

'Thanks.'

She went inside and I was left with Graham. I hoped he might say something but he had gone back to staring across the large pool and its small central island with its single rowan tree. I rehearsed to myself various things to say before remarking that they had a beautiful place.

He gave me a sideways glance that could only be called contemptuous.

'It's lucky no one's built any villas over there,' I said, pointing at the unspoilt vista. His battered mind was obviously on other things because he gave me another suspicious look, then stretched out a clawlike hand and with difficulty scooped up several salted almonds from the dish in front of him.

I helped myself to some and remarked how good they were.

'Very moreish,' I said with a laugh, but again I did not get through to him. I found myself wishing for Margot's return.

Suddenly, looking down at the remaining almond in the palm of his hand, he made a masticating movement with his lips and said in a low, confidential tone: 'Black olives — Kalamata are the best' — and he carefully placed the almond in the top pocket of his shirt.

'Did you manage to have a little chat?' Margot asked on her return. 'I thought I'd leave you alone for a while.'

'Maybe Graham would like some black olives,' I suggested.

She looked at me in surprise. 'No, he doesn't care for olives. Why, did he say something about them?'

'It doesn't matter,' I said and was grateful to find that she had been generous with the gin. She leant across to him and said gently, 'We're very silent this evening, aren't we? Enjoying your drink? Like it topped up a bit?'

He nodded and she turned to me and as she passed she mouthed to me with a conspiratorial smile, 'I'll add some more tonic.'

'It's a long time,' I said to him and took up my glass and held it between the palms of my hands, feeling the coldness of the ice.

A twisted smile lit up his face momentarily and I thought he was going to say something but he was interrupted by Margot's return.

'Have some more almonds,' she said to him and she handed him the bowl. 'The doctor says he's got to eat more than he does,' she said. 'He says it doesn't matter what, so long as he gets more into him.'

Graham carefully took three of the almonds out of the bowl with his right hand and placed them in the palm of his left.

'Jack's come all the way from London just to see you,' she said.

I gave her top marks for trying, though it seemed clear that for the moment Graham neither knew who Jack was nor why I should come from London to bother him by the poolside.

I found myself drinking more than I wanted, just to get through the evening.

'I've decided we'll have an early night,' Margot announced. 'Tomorrow's Sunday and we're having some friends in to lunch. They are people Graham has known for a long time.'

Roberto served us a cold meal out by the pool. By this time Graham was completely shut up inside himself, so Margot and I talked. She reminded me that when we had parted and she had married Graham we had agreed that we would keep in touch but somehow neither of us had the inclination to carry on a correspondence.

'At least I hope you're happy now?' she asked, as though it was I who had left her in some wild search for happiness.

'Not really,' I answered truthfully.

'Some of us are made to be happy, some not,' she said reflectively, 'and you, my dear, for all your talents, belong to the latter group.'

She was sitting at the head of the table, while I was on her right.

Suddenly, as though to interrupt the conversation I was having with Margot, Graham tipped his plate of salad and turkey breast on to the floor, while keeping his eyes fixed with unconcealed animosity on me.

'That's too bad of you, darling,' she said, and she

began crawling about under the table to collect the spilt food. I helped by gathering up some pieces of lettuce that had found their way on to one of my shoes.

'I'm afraid he's being particularly difficult today,' she apologized. 'I think maybe it's the excitement of your visit.'

We sat about for some time longer with after-dinner brandies, in which Graham did not participate, then she announced that she felt it was time she put him to bed.

'Don't stay up,' she said.

The three of us exchanged good-nights, and I wandered off with my topped-up glass of brandy to explore the grounds and reflect on the possible reason why she should have invited me for the weekend. I knew from experience that with Margot motives for anything she did were seldom clear-cut.

I slept badly. Perhaps at the back of my mind was the thought that there might be a gentle knock at my door once she had got Graham to bed.

The next day I rose late and was the first to settle alongside the pool, with a paperback I had bought at the airport but which I had not imagined I would have time to read. Margot and Graham joined me late. I thought she looked unusually strained and that the two of them were not in the best of moods. When Roberto appeared and took Graham off for what I discovered was his daily walk round the garden, Margot informed me that she'd had the devil of a job getting Graham to bed.

'Eventually I made up the other bed in his room and succeeded in getting him off to sleep,' she explained, then went on to say that the people she had invited to lunch would be turning up soon. 'It's a change for Graham and these are people he's known for a long time and with whom he feels at ease.'

The first to arrive were a couple, Peter and Peggy Musgrave. They were Americans, he a retired businessman. Graham clearly felt less constrained with them because he suddenly announced: 'Jack's my oldest friend.'

I was then asked the usual questions by the couple and I explained that he and I had been old friends and that I had at one time worked for him. I felt there was no point in mentioning that the main thing we had in common was Margot.

Later three more guests arrived: Sir Philip and Lady Something – he had been our ambassador in various Middle Eastern capitals. The last to arrive was a large, pleasantly overweight Dutchman, whose name I didn't catch, but who had the ability of treating Graham as though he were perfectly normal and of eliciting from him more responses than anyone else. With these additions to the party, Graham came temporarily to life and a bottle of champagne was opened. The effort, however, clearly took something out of him and soon he relapsed into his former moroseness, at which Margot decided it was time to have lunch served. This was done by Roberto and the maid who had served me breakfast in the room.

At dinner there were just the three of us. Margot explained that at night Graham preferred fish and we therefore had a meal of vichyssoise, grilled fish and boiled potatoes and crème brulée. The somewhat plain meal was accorded a flinty local white wine. Roberto served at table in an efficient way which suggested a guest helping out rather than the chauffeur doubling as waiter. We then took our drinks outside, where it was still warm enough to sit. Margot indicated to Roberto that he was free for the rest of the evening and could take the car if he so wished but should make himself available first thing in the morning to drive me to the airport.

For a while we sat in silence as the last of the evening swallows dipped and rose over the pool and the trees opposite rolled themselves into shadow. Margot had given Graham a large ball of blue plasticine which had been recommended by his doctor as something with which he could amuse himself while at the same time exercising his hand and arm muscles.

'Do you remember the squash games we used to have?' I suddenly thought of asking him.

The response was immediate: a crooked smile and a roguish upward look of the eyes. 'I jolly well do,' he answered, carefully choosing his words, 'but how did you always manage to... to...' – and he became confused in his search for the simple word.

'To win?' I suggested with a laugh.' Oh, not always.'

'There's a lovely little silver cup in the study which he won at school for squash,' said Margot, but for Graham the subject had been exhausted, though he did cast one or two sideways glances at me as though I were now worth trying to place.

'I think you've had enough of that' – and she took the brandy glass from him. As she helped him through the French windows into the lounge, she called back to me: 'Take your drink into the study, I'll be with you in half an hour or so.'

I left my brandy unfinished and went through into the house. The crowded shelves showed that Graham's range of reading had extended beyond the sort of popular literature favoured by those who regarded it as a pastime, a fill-in between making more money and counting up what was already there. I took down a first edition of *Brighton Rock* and refreshed my memory of its early excellence. It was significant that nothing had been added to the library for the last five years; Margot had never been a reader other than of magazines.

'I don't know what I'd do without Maria,' she said on her return, considerably later than she had predicted. 'Graham sometimes gets really fractious. Today I thought he'd never allow us to get him into his pyjamas – you'd have thought we were trying to murder him.'

She sat down wearily in the armchair opposite me, her glass in her hand. I got up and put a small table beside her.

'You still don't smoke?' she enquired, and when I said I didn't she asked me to go to the long drawer of the desk and get out the packet of cigarettes and matches. 'It's a pleasure I allow myself once he's safely tucked up in bed.'

I lit the cigarette for her, then looked around for an ashtray and brought it over from the window-sill.

'How did you find him?'

I made a grimace. 'I'm not sure what I expected. I suppose it's rather worse than I thought. What do the doctors say?'

'He has various pills,' she said, 'but I think they're more for me than for him. They're supposed to keep him calm. It's difficult to accept that he's just drifting and there's nothing to be done to stop him . . . stop him from going all the way.'

She looked away from me and drew on the cigarette.

'I'm sorry, Margot,' I said to her.

'Nobody can say it's not a bed I didn't make myself,' she remarked, glancing across at me and we both managed a laugh. 'The only good thing is that I think he's quite unaware of what's happening to him. Of course, as you can see, I don't lack for anything,' she went on. 'Even so it's not been exactly an easy life these last few years. When he started getting funny and forgetful and we eventually went to a doctor, I couldn't believe my ears – Graham who prided himself on keeping young, the man who never made any compromises with himself.'

I broke into her silence: 'Did he in fact ask to see me?'

'No,' she admitted.

I waited in the hope that she would say something more, but she remained silent, drawing nervously on the cigarette and blowing out clouds of smoke.

'I didn't think so – he didn't look as if he even knew who I was . . .'

'Oh, he mentions you sometimes – generally it's about something when you both first got to know each other. He can't tell you what he's had for dinner and then he'll suddenly come out with some story from years ago. The terrible thing is that sometimes I feel that the doctors are perhaps all wrong and that he's getting better, then he goes back to doing the oddest things, like peeing in his shoes or cutting up the sheets. No, I thought it might do him some good to see you, also I felt it might do something for me. You see, Jack, I'm awfully alone in all this. You saw most of our friends at lunch. The only one I really care for is old Honegger, he's a delightful person and a rock of comfort, but he's got his own agenda in all this . . .'

'Oh yes?' I said archly.

'He's a widower and has always had a soft spot for me.'

'You wouldn't presumably be doing Graham out of anything?' She nodded. 'And you're not the girl for the celibate life.'

'Funnily enough, though he's got his eye on me, I don't think in the circumstances he'd want to have an affair with me. He'd like me to be Mrs Honegger – and he's just about the richest man this side of Cannes.'

'And Roberto?' I couldn't help asking.

'He's dishy enough,' she answered, 'but he's a bit obvious – also, my dear, one doesn't go to bed with one's chauffeur.'

She took another cigarette and I got to my feet and struck a match.

'I'm sorry, Margot,' I said and squeezed her shoulder.

'I know you are,' she said. 'In some ways, Jack, you've always been a very magnanimous person . . . After all, you have every right to say that I had it coming to me.'

'Oh, if we all got our deserts, as someone said, who would escape a hanging?'

'And you?' she asked. 'Written any good books lately?'

'People say we've all got one good book inside us – perhaps I wrote mine fifteen years back. But even that one didn't really make it.'

'What was it called?' She looked around her as

though the title was hovering just within reach.

'I was hurt that she couldn't remember. *The Woman Named Tomorrow* — it's a quotation from the American poet Carl Sandburg.'

'Oh yes,' she said. 'It was really very good. Maybe it came out at the wrong time.'

'At least it got into paperback. It came up for review the other day but they decided not to reprint.' I shrugged my shoulders. 'I'm writing something at the moment but I have to do so much hack work to keep the wolves from the door that I don't have all that amount of time.'

'And your other interest in life?'

I darted a glance at her and saw that she meant what I thought she meant.

'Nothing I wouldn't trade in for writing an acceptable novel.'

She gave a deep sigh and said: 'It's a stupid life. I hope you believe me that I didn't marry him for his money.'

'You didn't just marry him, you left me to do it — and I was very fond of you.'

'Sometimes you didn't show it sufficiently.'

'I suppose I'd never thought of Graham as a possible rival. Perhaps I should have done.'

'He gave me a sense of security — and I don't mean just financial.'

'In fact he made the greater part of his wealth after he married you,' I reminded her.

'That's right,' she said.

'And he left poor... what was her name?'

'Susan,' she supplied. 'She married again and suddenly started having babies, something that Graham never seemed able to supply his women with.'

'Are you sorry – about yourself, I mean?'

'Not having children?' She seemed to consider the question, then shook her head. 'No, having an incontinent husband has rather cured me of such instincts. Anyway, it's all water under the bridge, as they say.'

'And why didn't we have one?' I found myself asking.

'Because you always said you didn't want children and I was too honest not to respect your wishes.'

'I suppose I felt there wasn't enough money,' I pointed out.

'There never is,' she said.

'It's the lot of most of us. Only a few own places in the South of France with Mercedes cars and all that goes with them.'

'So what?' she said. 'It doesn't stop one being as lonely as a dog – or you could say bitch if you liked' – and she gave a twisted smile, a smile I knew so well, a smile that said, 'I know all this looks very histrionic, but I really am playing it honest and straight.'

As she looked up at me the lamplight caught the tears that had welled up in her eyes. Then, like a droplet hanging from a tap, a tear trickled down her cheek. I had seen Margot cry often and generally I was the cause and it always made me feel sad and guilty – and also physically loving.

I walked across to her and put a hand on her shoulder. The action brought more tears coursing down her face. 'I'm sorry.' She gave me her cigarette and indicated I should stub it out. When I seated myself on the arm of the chair she put her arm behind my neck and brought my head down to meet her lips. I tasted the alcohol, the smokiness of her mouth and the salt of tears. The taste of tears always excited me. The thought went through my mind that I had no one to be faithful to. Together we took off her panties and she lowered her body in the chair and passed me a cushion. As I entered her all she said was, 'Ah, I wanted that,' and gave a little gasp of joy. When we finished she passed her hand over my damp forehead in a gesture of tenderness.

It was I who first noticed the figure of Graham, dressed in white pyjamas, standing by the open door of the study, the darkness of the corridor behind him. She followed my gaze. I moved aside and she brushed down her skirt and hurriedly rose to her feet.

'Oh, you are a naughty boy. Can't you sleep, darling?' and she took him by the arm and led him out of the room.

I stuffed her panties into my jacket pocket and

sipped at the remains of the green Chartreuse she had been drinking. I waited for twenty minutes but she didn't return.

Once again I slept badly. I was worried as to what Graham had seen or overheard, and whether in fact his mind was capable of taking in the significance of the scene he had witnessed. Did it matter? I kept asking myself. As she herself had said, she was not depriving him of anything. What I wanted, though, at that moment, was her presence, also an assurance from her, however brief, that what had happened had meant more to her than the simple satisfying of a physical need. What, too, I wanted to ask her, was her real reason for having her first husband spend this weekend with his ex-wife and her ailing husband?

I again breakfasted in my room. When I went downstairs I found Graham seated in his usual chair by the pool. I approached him with trepidation but he appeared to be in a more friendly mood. He even motioned to the water as though to suggest that I might have a dip – or that is what I supposed.

'I'm afraid I'm leaving this morning.'

'Must you?' he said.

'I'm expected back at my job.'

I waited in vain for Margot.

Eventually Roberto came towards us and informed me that Mrs Didcot wasn't feeling well and asked to be excused. Was I packed and ready to go to the airport?

I wrote her a 'thank–you' letter and waited hopefully for a reply. It was four months later that I received a brief note telling me that Graham had died of a stroke. I wrote back offering my condolences, also any help I could give her. Her reply to that letter came only two months later; in it she informed me that she would be marrying Mr Honegger – 'You may remember he was there at lunch on the Sunday.' For some time I kept asking myself if things would have turned out differently had Graham not made his appearance in the doorway that night. In the meantime, I keep making changes to my novel and putting off sending it to a publisher.

12
A Smile from the Past

It was a sunny morning and the forecast was that it would remain fine for the whole day with a slight westerly breeze. Matron had asked him if he'd like to sit out for a while, so the Jamaican nurse he insisted on calling Sarah had helped him down the steps into the garden where a chair had been placed alongside the hedge that acted as a wind-break. Sarah tucked a rug round him and gave him the information that there was chocolate mousse for lunch.

'Good,' he said, though slightly irritated at himself for showing interest in the contents of the meals that stood as milestones along his barren days. Earlier that morning he had tried to stop himself from commenting that his bacon hadn't been done to the crispness he liked.

'You can have a quiet snooze till it's coffee time,' said Sarah, leaning over him and talking into his left – his *good* – ear.

'I don't want to have a quiet snooze, or even a noisy one for that matter,' he said gruffly, though he was fond of Sarah. 'I'd like my *Times*.'

'I'll bring it,' she said, and he was conscious of her ample presence moving away from him.

He must have dropped off for a while, because when he was woken by a shaft of sunlight that peeped through his half-closed lids, he found his hands folded over the copy of *The Times*. As often happened, he hadn't slept well that night. For the last ten years or so, in fact ever since he'd come to the home, he'd have a sort of twilight sleep till nearly dawn, then suddenly drop into total unconsciousness for the last hour or two. It was generally with a shock that he awoke seemingly only seconds before there was a knock at his door and one of the nurses came in and helped him with his pillow and put the breakfast tray on the bedside table. The shock was doubtless the same as that suffered by those in prison under sentence of death: people who awake each morning to a reality that is painful and has to be accepted anew each day. In his case he awakened to the fact that he was an old man and an inmate in a home for old people. This sudden flood of knowledge always made him frightened and slightly breathless. The feeling was particularly distressing if, as often happened in that period of late deep sleep, he had dreamt about himself leading a younger and more active life. Generally in these dreams he would be back in his *shamba* in the White Highlands of Kenya. When the Mau Mau troubles had started he had felt he should do the right thing and send his wife Gwen back to England. He himself had stayed on, happy enough despite the difficulties and dangers, and when he'd written to her to come out again and join him, it seemed she'd got used to life in England, or perhaps had found somebody else. It didn't come as a surprise to him when she eventually wrote and asked for a divorce. When the work on the *shamba* had got too much for him he'd been persuaded by a neighbour to sell up and go back to England, and for a while he had lived in a small cottage in a pretty Hampshire village. But he missed the wide vistas of Kenya and now had little memory of the cottage except for the coldness of the winters and the loneliness of feeling that he didn't belong.

Often in his dreams he would find himself speaking Kikuyu to the boys, though in his waking hours he was not conscious of having retained any words of the language. A recurrent dream showed one of the boys walking along with a *debe* of water that knocked awkwardly against his bare muscular legs. For the first few paces water splashed over the sides and left dark splotches in the dry earth. This was then replaced by a single trickle of water and the realization that the *debe* was leaking. He would shout at the boy, who merely grinned back at him and continued on his way to the bed of zinnias. Striding over to the boy, he would wrench the *debe* from him, by which time it was almost empty. He then rested it on the ground and watched helplessly as the remaining water oozed away.

He forced himself to take up *The Times* and glance over the items on the front page. As usual he found nothing of interest. Though he continued to order *The Times* – it was a matter of pride to him that he was the only one in the home who took it – he read scarcely more than the larger headlines. Whole sections of it seemed now to be devoted to matters which, even in his younger days, were of little interest to him, like sports and finance, and the only items of world news that he read through in full were the occasional ones about Africa, mainly of coups, unrest and famine. He looked at the TV programmes for the evening, noting which ones were recommended, and glanced at the obituaries and deaths, though sometimes ruefully reminding himself that all the people he knew who might feature had died long ago. Only very occasionally would he find a letter on the correspondence page that aroused his indignation or mirth. Even the crossword puzzle, which he had always enjoyed, was now beyond him. There was a time when he was invariably able to complete the greater part of it, seldom leaving more than the odd corner unfilled. Of course in the home there wasn't room for all his reference books, so he was no longer able to look up some quotation from Shelley or Wordsworth. Sometimes – a year or two back now – he'd keep that day's crossword and look at the solution the following morning, but more and more frequently he found the clues far-fetched or unfathomable. It seemed to him that the persons setting the crosswords had been changed and that he was somehow not on their wavelength.

Sometimes he missed his personal belongings. Once he'd told Sarah about his wonderful collection of books and records and for days after he felt hollow with the loss of them. The first jettisoning had been when he had sold up the *shamba* in Kenya; he had left many of his prized books and records behind, not having the energy or the tea chests in which to pack them, though for some reason he had taken back with him his entire stock of khaki shorts and shirts, only to throw them away once he'd settled into his cottage. Then, having sold the cottage when his daughter and her solicitor husband persuaded him he was no longer able to look after himself, he had disposed of the remainder of his books – with the exception of a copy of the *Bible*, the *Concise Oxford Dictionary* and a one-volume edition of Shakespeare, whose print was now far too small for him. With the proceeds from the cottage his son-in-law had negotiated for him a room of his own for the term of his life in

Bolding Heights. The room was long and narrow and held a bed, an armchair and a small table under the window that supported a 9-inch television set in case he didn't feel like joining the others in the TV room. On his dressing-table he had a faded photograph of his mother and father and a small reproduction of W.J. Mahler's portrait of Beethoven; the photograph of his daughter he brought out and stood alongside Beethoven when she and her husband visited him on his birthday. He also owned a small radio and a pair of headphones so that during his hours of sleeplessness he could listen without disturbing anyone; often of a morning he would be found fast asleep, still wearing them, which would be a source of amusement to the nurses.

Holding the paper awkwardly, his outstretched arms growing heavy with the effort, he peeked at each spread, momentarily enjoying the picture of a leopard with her cubs in some European zoo, and then folded it up and let his eyes run down the crossword clues. He was about to cast it aside and doze off till morning coffee was brought when he read 'A great lady launcher' (5) and was immediately able to write in 'Helen'. He went through all the clues again, lingering longer over each one, especially those that contained letters from 'Helen', but nothing else came to mind.

He was replacing the cap on his Biro when the name 'Helen' edged itself into the recesses of his brain. Like a piece of grit in an oyster shell, it set up an irritation and demanded his attention. He lay back in the chair and, working from experience, allowed the name to float about weightlessly between the walls of his head. After three-quarters of a lifetime of being submerged, a vignette, bright and pristine as the day it had been lived, rose up from the slime of his subconscious:

In a cramped ship's cabin a woman sat in front of a mirror. She was wrapped round in a towel that left her breasts bare, while he lay propped up on the bunk behind her and watched the almost black rosettes of her breasts rising and falling as she brushed her hair. The brush had steel bristles fixed into a red rubber base. Passing his tongue over his dry lips, he mouthed the name 'Helen' and she smiled at him in the mirror and said, 'Happy?' while the fan revolved slowly in the becalmed air of Port Sudan.

Sarah nudged him back into the garden at Bolding Heights. 'Coffee,' she said brightly. 'Sit up now. Upsy-daisy.' He took the cup from her and nursed it in his lap. Once she had turned away he managed to bend over and put it on the grass beside him. Following her large rump as she walked back to the house, he remembered her once telling him that he had at least got his memories. She'd meant it as a kindly remark but it had only served to remind him that his time for living had ceased, that all he had left was the experience of reliving memories, and these were, day by day, being whittled away. Constantly, by conscious effort, they had to be rescued from the *oubliettes* to which old age condemned them one by one and to which the jailers of the mind ventured ever more infrequently.

He stirred and the newspaper slipped from his lap. As he leaned over to pick it up he noticed his coffee beside him and saw that it had grown a discoloured coating. He stirred it with the butt of his pen and drank down half of it with a grimace.

In order to underline that Helen was no mere clue in a crossword puzzle, he wrote her name in large capital letters down the margin of the back page: H–E–L–E–N. He felt triumphant: somehow, by some miracle, he had clawed back from the darkness of his mind a memory, the memory of perhaps one of the most important moments of his life. How, of all his memories, had it been allowed to sink almost beyond the reach of recall? Had the vagaries of the mind consigned it, for reasons of its own (perhaps, at the time, to spare it pain?) to seeming oblivion?

He tried to concentrate his mind on the name Helen, almost physically seeking to squeeze into existence further scenes. Had he known her before meeting her on the ship? Had she too joined it at Tilbury? What had happened between there and Port Sudan? Had she perhaps disembarked a few days later at Aden? If at Mombasa, was there a husband awaiting her? Why had not more come of their relationship? Was it because at the time he had been engaged to be married and his fiancée was booked to follow him out to Kenya?

He became aware of Sarah's presence beside him, of her picking up the paper from his lap.

'"Helen?"' he heard her say in her singsong voice. 'Is that all you've been able to do?' He kept his eyes closed. 'And you've not finished your coffee,' she said, her voice raised several octaves in mock scolding.

And then to his irritation she slowly read out the clue.

'What makes you think Helen's right?' she asked, then bent down and picked up the cup. Before she left she affectionately touched the old man on the shoulder.

Of course Helen was right.

Behind his closed eyelids lay the tropic heat and pungent smell of foreign ports. A half-naked woman was smiling at him in a mirror as she brushed her hair with rhythmic strokes. Against the noise of the ceiling fan came the monotonous worksong of the stevedores as they followed each other up the narrow, bending planks into the bowels of the ship. The faceless black stevedores, their bare backs glistening, moved as on a conveyor-belt. Above their chanting he could hardly hear Helen asking her question: 'Happy?'

Sweet Helen.

13
A Taxi to Himself

A young Englishman with long fair hair is standing
by a newspaper kiosk. He is wearing a grey
corduroy jacket, loose khaki trousers and a red
check shirt. He stands several feet into the road so
that the traffic rushes past him dangerously close.
Behind him on the pavement sit several black-
clothed peasant women with baskets beside them
or babies supported on their shoulders; they talk in
loud, raucous voices as though quarrelling. The
young man's eyes rove among the four lanes of
traffic as they advance on him on their way up Giza
Street which begins several miles away at the
Pyramids; the bulk of it will cross the bridge at the
Sheraton Hotel and make its way over a second
bridge to Liberation Square and the city centre;

179

some of it will turn left at the first bridge and follow the river in the direction of Zamalek.

From time to time the young man darts amidst the lanes of traffic calling out 'At-Tahreer' (which in Arabic means 'Liberation') to any taxi in which he has spotted a spare seat. By this expedient he tells the driver that his own destination is Maidan at-Tahreer or Liberation Square. As they race past him some of the passengers turn in his direction and stare blankly or smile. From time to time, too, he shifts the many books he is carrying from under one arm to under the other; some are thin and have the habit of sliding out between the bigger books. From time to time he glances at his watch, more a nervous tic than a real wish to know the time. He is unprepared when a taxi carrying a lone girl in the back drives straight at him. He jumps to one side and at the same moment several of the women behind him break into laughter. The taxi screeches to a halt; the girl leans forward and pays the driver. As she closes the door and turns round he thinks he recognizes one of his students, but she doesn't glance at him.

Hesitant, as though fearful of his good luck, he enquires of the driver: 'Maidan at-Tahreer?'

The driver nods and the Englishman gets in beside him. The Englishman glances sideways at the driver and finds him to be a bull-necked man in perhaps his fifties with a greying fringe of beard. In front of him, dangling from the mirror by a leather thong, is a miniature copy of the Qur'an, while stuck along the dashboard are various injunctions about honouring one's parents, putting one's trust in Allah and being beware of the envious.

The Englishman settles the books in his lap and gazes out of the window at the tall iron gateway into the Russian Embassy where the taxi, having taken the inner lane, has come to a stop behind a white Mercedes with diplomatic number plates and a black chauffeur with a cap. On top of the pile of books lies a Samuel Beckett paperback that the Englishman has nearly finished reading. The sight of the author's name puts him in mind of the many combinations that constitute the unwritten law on where to sit in one of Cairo's taxis if you are lucky enough to find one. Seeing the long line of traffic in front of them, the Englishman sets about enumerating in his mind the rules to be followed:

If one is a man on his own and – as in the present, highly rare case – the taxi is empty, one should, unless one is a snob or doesn't mind being thought one, take the seat next to the driver; one also, of course – even though a snob – takes the same seat if there should happen to be a woman in the back. If the front seat is taken (by a man) and there is a lone woman in the back, then the man in the front gives up his place to the woman and he and the newly arrived passenger will share the back. If it happens that the front seat is taken by a woman, then she will move back with the other woman, giving up her seat beside the driver to the new passenger. If two men join the taxi and it happens to be empty, it is legitimate for them to sit together in the back, though sometimes one of them will sit in front with the driver and a three-cornered conversation will ensue; if there's a woman in the back, she will be invited to the front and the two men will occupy the rear seat. If you're a woman and the taxi's empty, you sit at the back; if there's another woman at the back, you join her; if there's a man — or two men — in the back, you sit next to the driver. If two women are waiting, they will, if the taxi is empty, sit together at the back; if occupied by another woman then they will all squeeze in together; if there's a lone man sitting beside the driver, that's all right, but if he's a snob and sitting alone in the back and doesn't of himself get out and move up front, the driver will ask him to vacate his seat to the two women. It is all based, the Englishman tells himself, on the Prophetic Saying that where a man and a woman are alone together the Devil makes a third, though it would seem that taxi drivers provide an exception to the rule.

The young Englishman wonders whether there are any other combinations and the thought strikes him that no doubt Beckett's Molloy would have found one or more. He then tells himself that he must make a point of asking one of his Egyptian literary friends whether anyone has yet made an attempt to translate Beckett into Arabic. He becomes aware that the taxi has moved on and is now waiting alongside the entrance to the Sheraton Hotel. He watches three Japanese in dark business suits bowing at each other as the uniformed doorman holds the door open for them. As none will take the initiative, two elderly American women dressed in green trouser-suits pass through the door simultaneously and shoulder their way between the three Japanese men.

As the taxi jerks into motion the Englishman notices that the driver has opened a new packet of Marlboro cigarettes. He crumples up the cellophane wrapping and drops it out of the window, followed by the loose piece of silver paper. He extends the open packet towards the Englishman.

'Thanks, I don't smoke,' the Englishman answers in Arabic, having already prepared the phrase in his mind. With his free hand the driver changes gear and moves off again. He lights the cigarette carefully from the remaining match, gives the box a final shake and throws it out. The Englishman, feeling that the driver's gesture of generosity requires of him to keep the conversation going, says: 'I'm trying to give it up.'

The driver expresses surprise and admiration, then says that he too has tried several times to give it up. He explains that he finds his job nerve-racking and that smoking is a help. He looks sideways at the Englishman: 'Petrol for the car and cigarettes for me.' The two men laugh.

They're now passing across the bridge with the hotel to their right. Two fishing boats lie below the hotel; in one of them a man is lifting up a length of net, examining it, then lifting up another length. In the other boat a woman suckles a child, while a young girl dips a can into the river and pours water over her feet.

Traffic has built up on the bottle-neck of the bridge. Two police officers run between the lines of traffic blowing whistles and gesticulating. Some of the drivers blow their horns out of boredom. The taxi draws up behind a bus, which continues to spew out a black scarf of smoke. The Englishman hastily winds up his window.

'You speak Arabic well,' says the taxi driver, and the Englishman explains that he studied Arabic before coming out to Egypt. The driver asks him what he works at, where he lives, whether he has a family in Cairo. Then the driver asks whether he can read and write Arabic. 'A bit,' says the Englishman. 'Have you read the Qur'an?' asks the taxi driver.

The Englishman is trying to say that he has started to study some of the Qur'an with the brother of one of his students who has studied at the religious university of al-Azhar. The driver is nodding his head approvingly when one of two girls, dressed in a form of uniform with wide-brimmed hats and holding cartons of locally manufactured paper handkerchiefs, approaches the driver. He waves her away roughly and the Englishman fails to understand what he shouts at her or her ribald reply.

'The government shouldn't allow it,' says the driver. 'They're like prostitutes walking about the streets – and the handkerchiefs they sell aren't any good.'

'I suppose they can't get any other work,' says the Englishman in their defence.

'They should be sitting at home and not wandering the streets and showing their legs.'

'Yes,' says the Englishman, realizing from the tone of voice that this is a subject the driver feels strongly about. Ahead of them he watches a man, whom he's seen on previous occasions, hopping on one leg between the cars. He is without arms. He stops alongside the chauffeur of a large black car with smoked rear windows. The chauffeur shakes his head and turns away but is then handed a note from the back – the Englishman briefly sees a braceleted arm – so he presses a button and lowers his window and places the fifty-piastre note among the others that protrude from the front pocket in the man's shirt. The man immediately looks around him sizing up the other cars and their occupants. Seeing the Englishman, he hesitates, then rejects him and hops between the taxi and the bus to a new BMW holding a young man at the wheel, a young woman beside him and an older woman in the back. The three occupants consult together and the man puts a pound note in the beggar's pocket. The Englishman fears that he will be the next person to be approached and feels embarrassed at the beggar's almost total disablement. He shifts the pile of books slightly, the more easily to penetrate his trouser pocket. Ahead there are signs that the traffic is again on the move and the driver puts the palm of his hand on the horn and keeps it there. At that moment a young man appears at the Englishman's window. The Englishman looks through the glass at the man – he is of a similar age to himself and could well be one of his students. He has a handsome, well–fed face and a tall muscular body. He is dressed in a white shirt with long sleeves, beige trousers with a black belt and sandals; his clothes are in no way shabby though slightly inadequate for the time of year. The young man meets the Englishman's hostile gaze and makes a movement with his right hand towards his mouth. The Englishman shakes his head while the driver of the taxi scrabbles among the loose change in front of him and produces a twenty-five piastre note. The Englishman lowers his window and passes on the money. The young man takes it without a word, puts it in his trouser pocket and moves off.

The Englishman, feeling guilty at not having given anything, remonstrates with the driver. He points out that the man is young and apparently healthy and should be earning a living.

'Who but Allah knows the circumstances of His creatures,' says the driver. 'We give for Allah's sake and He rewards for the intention.'

The Englishman understands only the first part of what the driver has said, but he ponders the words. As the traffic begins to move again he sees the hopping figure of the crippled beggar; the young man he has refused is not in sight.

'It is not for man to judge,' the driver adds, warming to the subject. 'Only Allah sees into the hearts of men.'

'You're right,' says the Englishman and twists round in his seat, steadying the pile of books with one hand and groping in his trouser pocket. He takes out a coin, which happens to be a ten–piastre piece, and passes it to the driver. 'Give it to him.'

Edging forward slowly, the driver sees the young man in his mirror. The young man is making the same gesture of putting his hand to his mouth to one of two girls sitting in the back of a taxi; she is embarrassed and turns to the other girl and starts talking.

The Englishman hears the taxi driver call to the young man. The driver's hand, holding a cigarette and the coin, lolls out of the window. Through the back side–window behind the driver the Englishman sees the young man walk out into the space between the taxi and an open lorry carrying workmen clinging to the sides when a motor cycle accelerates through the gap and strikes the young man from behind. He is lifted and hurled through the air into the back of a van standing in front of the lorry. The cyclist falls clear and the taxi driver brakes abruptly and the Englishman's books fall to the floor. By his action the taxi driver has prevented his left rear wheel from crushing the cyclist's legs. The cyclist picks himself up and examines a bleeding elbow and a tear in his trouser leg. He then rights his motor cycle and assures himself it's undamaged. The Englishman looks around him for the young man to whom he had intended to give the ten piastres and who had been hurled through the air into the back of the van. He sees him crouched in the road as though over a lavatory bowl. He is coughing up blood that is staining one of the sleeves of his white shirt.

The Englishman sees the lorry driver and his mate jump down and carry the young man by his shoulders and feet and lay him down on the pavement. The Englishman feels slightly faint and begins groping about for his books. The lines of traffic move slowly forward, out of sight of the body on the pavement.

The taxi driver hands back the ten-piastre piece. The two men avoid each other's eyes. The Englishman can see the driver's hands shake as he lights a fresh cigarette from a new box of matches.

14
Oleanders Pink and White

He had been driving since early morning. Now the blood-orange sun had climbed out of the greyness of dawn and stood dominant and aggressively golden in its pale-blue cradle. He drove the Land-Rover fast, following the serrated tracks made by previous vehicles. Sometimes, given a choice, he would swing sideways and change to another set of tracks that promised a faster ride. Though he was in no hurry, he enjoyed speeding across the expanse of *sabkha* that separated the low-lying range of mountains from a sea that blended almost imperceptibly with the sky. With a single hand on the steering-wheel, sometimes with no more than a finger, he guided the Land-Rover out of the way of boulders and the larger potholes. Catching sight of a black object against the monotonous landscape, he changed direction. As he passed the bloated body of a goat the cab filled with the stench and he cleared his throat and spat out of the window.

In the cold half-light of dawn he had showered and he could still feel the tingle of salt water on his body. It gave him a feeling of well-being, heady lightness. For the last ten days he had been on the other coast, ten days and nights spent at sea on one of the company's survey boats. It had been a time without beer and his mouth felt clean and fresh. For the first time since he'd come to the Gulf he'd had a taste of that life of adventure for which he had sacrificed the comfort of home with evenings at the pub and all the women you could manage. He told himself that it had taken guts to leave the familiar and the comfortable. The company had flown him out to Dubai and he'd been surprised to find it a baffling network of six-lane highways that looked like something out of an American film. Now, during this last ten days, he had had the chance of taking the place of a crew member who had gone down sick. At last he was having the sort of experience he had been seeking when he'd applied for the job with the oil company.

He had enjoyed working on the survey boat in the heat of the Indian Ocean. The job he had in Dubai with the oil company as an assistant storekeeper wasn't much fun but it paid good money and was all found, so he was stashing away quite a bit, even with the beer he was drinking. Money meant a good time, also freedom. He remembered being told that by a young fellow in a pub back home and the fact that he'd drunk no more than a bitter lemon and then driven off in a Ferrari engrained the remark in his mind.

During his time at sea he'd done some snorkelling and one of the lads noticed he was a powerful swimmer and had given him a couple of lessons in diving with oxygen cylinders. Then someone said something about a place up in Scotland where you could take a course in diving and get qualified for a job on one of the North Sea rigs or with a company anywhere in the world with an offshore concession. It seemed that getting oil out of the seabed was the coming thing and there was big money for experienced divers. The instructor said he was getting on fine but that he should be careful not to be over-confident. He nearly told him where to get off but held his tongue and instead invited him to go out for a drink when he was next in Dubai. You never knew what a good word from such a man could do for you.

But if his days on the boat had done anything for him it was to confirm that there was something about him that gave him the edge on other lads. He had always kept himself fit, even though he liked his beer and was one for the women. Before coming out to the Gulf he'd thought of joining the SAS or one of those special outfits they showed you about on the telly. But he reckoned he wouldn't care for the sort of discipline they had. No way would he be told every second of the day where to go and what to do. No, he wouldn't say he was over-confident exactly, just that if he really wanted something he'd got the guts to go after it. He knew that his mates felt this, too, even if some of them resented it. One night they'd all been drinking in the Staff House and somebody said of him, 'Danny couldn't care a fuck.' Yes, that just about summed it up, he reckoned, and he grinned at the recollection.

As he drove, his thoughts were on the evening that lay ahead. He'd more than make up for the ten days he'd just had without a drink. He'd take himself out for a slap-up meal, perhaps at one of the big hotels along the creek, and see if he couldn't pick up some girl, then end up with a beer session at the Staff House. Tomorrow was Friday and he could sleep it off the whole day. He tried to remember how many cartons of beer he'd got stacked up at the Staff House. These last few days he hadn't been using his rations and he was due for a new lot at the beginning of the month. Just so long as none of the lads had been dipping into his supplies. Not twice they wouldn't – and he laughed out loud. It was a great thing having everything all found and nothing to spend your money on except beer and cigarettes, and both of these didn't come cheaper than out here. There was only one thing missing: crumpet. He remembered one of the older men expressing the view that crumpet wasn't everything and he, answering quick as a flash, saying 'Isn't it?' and all the lads rolling about in their seats and trying not to spew up their beer. Some of the boys had it off with a Lebanese bint who operated from a flat near the Clock Tower on Deira side, but he didn't fancy paying for it. 'You never get a purr out of paid pussy,' he'd thought up on the spur of the moment and ever since, if someone wanted to raise a laugh, they had only to repeat the phrase. In a couple of months he was due for local leave: maybe he'd go to Cyprus, or even all the way to Bangkok where they said there was all the crumpet you could want just for taking them out for a meal and perhaps giving them some little present.

For the time being he would have to do with beer, and he savoured in his mind the ice-cold touch of the tin rim against his lips and the breathtaking gulps taken from the first can drunk out of sheer thirst. The first two were the best, then there was that long haul up to the crossroads, when you knew from experience that you either called a halt or you continued on your journey to oblivion so that it was only the next morning that your mates told you how they'd got you home and put you to bed and the arguments and fights you'd got yourself into.

He followed the coastline with the empty sea to his left, occasionally passing small plantations of date-palms, or straggly lime trees surrounded by rough cane barriers against stray goats and the sand that scudded across the open desert. The morning breeze that had started bitingly cold now ballooned out his shirt and laid a clammy, sandpaper hand on his chest. As he drew nearer to the stage cut-out of mountains ahead, he bore inland, his foot hard down on the accelerator. The roar of the engine in the surrounding emptiness drummed in his brain, cocooning him in a world of which he felt himself to be in total control.

Ahead, the monotony of the landscape was broken by the angular outline of three camels. On the leading two he could make out riders swaying to the loping gait. Behind the second camel was a third, riderless and led by a nose-rope. He wondered where they were bound and the thought came to him that not many years ago there was no other form of transport in these parts. Didn't they call them 'ships of the desert'? He remembered the book he'd found lying around at the Staff House by someone who'd crossed the Empty Quarter: descriptions of the heat and the feel of burning sand underfoot and going for days without water and in the evening having wrestling matches with his Bedouin companions. He felt sadness at the thought he'd missed out on things like that.

Without slackening speed he turned the Land-

Rover sharply, the back wheels slithering on the crust of *sabkha*; he let go of the steering-wheel and the car followed the skid in a zigzag, then headed for the file of camels. He drove it hard across well-worn tracks and he had to hold on to the steering-wheel with both hands as the car juddered in protest. It was like riding some restive horse that had to be strictly curbed. He glanced sideways and saw the man on the leading camel turn round and gesture to his companion. They didn't change pace or direction, but now both men were watching the fast-approaching Land-Rover.

Just to disappear, he told himself; just to abandon the Land-Rover in the desert and get on to that third camel and accompany the Arabs to whatever destination they were heading for. He would live it rough with them, would — like the man in the book — sleep alongside them in a hollow in the sand, existing on a few handfuls of dates and sips of brackish water, then suddenly, perhaps weeks later, turn up at the Staff House, bearded and dressed in Arab robes and carrying one of those long hooked canes that marked you out as a man of the desert, a nomad for whom everywhere and nowhere is home.

He was approaching them at right angles and grinned to himself at the look of alarm on the faces of the two men. He braked, changed down and slewed the Land-Rover round at the last moment in a cloud of dust.

'*Salaam aleikum*,' he called and waved at the two men and they raised their hands in reply. He took a packet of Rothmans from the carton beside him. '*Hie!*' he shouted and he threw it up into the air, then let in the clutch and raced back towards the tracks he had left. As the dust cleared he saw the men in his mirror: they were continuing on their way as though they hadn't seen him throw out the packet. 'Silly fuckers!' he exclaimed out loud. By now he had forgotten about the idea of joining them and going off to the Empty Quarter: all he felt was contempt for them and resentment at their rejection of his generosity.

A dip in the cardboard-cut-out line of mountains indicated the location of the small wadi through which he had been told he had to pass before he reached the made-up road that would bring him to the other coast, to the townships of Sharjah and Dubai. Again he glanced in the mirror and smiled as he saw one of the men dismount from his kneeling camel and walk back to pick up the cigarettes. 'Not such silly fuckers after all!' he told himself and laughed out loud, happy in the thought that with this one spontaneous act he had succeeded in making contact with these simple desert people. For most Westerners, for the others at the Staff House for instance, ragged Bedouin were nothing but part of a landscape, no more approachable than the rocks and the scrub and occasional stunted thorn bush. With him, though, he knew that it would take no time before he was speaking their language and was accepted by them as someone capable of enduring the hardships and dangers of their life. Some time maybe, he mused, instead of lying on his bed and reading thrillers, he'd stroll down to the lines of dhows moored in Dubai creek and choose one of them and make his way to Zanzibar or somewhere, living rough on deck with a bunch of Arabs and Baluchis.

He groped under the seat and brought out a thermos of icy water. He drank from it without slowing down and some of the water splashed down his chest making his shirt cling tightly to him. He poured water into the palm of his hand and sprinkled it down the back of his neck. At once, sweat began to trickle down his forehead and he had to take off his sunglasses and wipe them against his khaki shorts.

The mountain range ahead threw jagged shadows that pointed seawards. Above, the sun was set like a boil in an unclouded sky. The entrance to the wadi bed was partly obscured by an outcrop of rock. Only the convergence of several tyre tracks indicated where lay the way through. He changed down as the Land-Rover's wheels met the larger stones that occasional rains had washed down. He had to content himself with negotiating the narrow stretch of boulder-strewn track at a walking pace. Then the defile broadened out into an area of pebbled river-bed with several clumps of oleander bushes growing in a patch of sand among discarded tyres and rusting tins. The wadi had been dry for months but some of the oleanders were in bloom with white, others with faded pink, flowers. The squat forms of goats moved jerkily among the bushes, then panicked at his approach and scampered farther up the ravine. He brought the car to a halt and with the action of shutting off the engine created a sudden vacuum of silence. For several seconds he remained seated, his ears slowly clearing of sound. He stared about him: at the dozen or so goats that were back browsing among the stones, the pebbled watercourse, and the unlikely clumps of oleanders that grew and even flowered in this barrenness.

He placed a cigarette between his lips; when he clicked the lighter, he could scarcely make out the flame against the furnace of sunlight. 'Jesus, it's hot,' he said, and his words and the smoke he puffed out hung about in the still air. Would the two men and their camels be passing this way? More likely they would strike inland to the coast and make their way by Fujairah into Oman. His mind lingered on them for a while as he blew out more smoke. He formed a picture of himself riding the leading camel, the two Arabs following.

He got out of the car and looked around him, the cigarette held loosely in his mouth, his hands on his hips. He took a step to the front of the car, slipped his hand inside his shorts and pulled them aside. He watched the almost invisible jet of urine strike against the tyre. On an impulse he took the cigarette from his mouth with the other hand and held the burning tip in the path of the arc. It sizzled and he let it drop. He gave a sigh of satisfaction and straightened up. 'That's better.' The words broke into the silence and gave him a sense of being in command of the emptiness around him.

Standing, his hands back on his hips, watching the robotlike movements of the goats, he became aware of the burning of the sun on the back of his neck. Something scuttled among the pebbles at his feet and a sudden breathlessness of panic was replaced by a relaxation of his tensed muscles as he made out the intricate lustre of a lizard flickering to a lifeless stop beside his foot, its bright eyes staring out at the sun's disc. An unexplained sense of unease, of being encompassed by the walls of the miniature wadi, probed at his confidence and he looked down at his feet to make sure that what he had seen was nothing more than a lizard. He had heard tales of the snakes that abounded in the desert, some of the smaller ones being the most dangerous.

As he moved towards the door of the car some of the goats started scampering up the water-course with explosive farting noises and the thought came to him that someone must be in charge of them. He turned quickly and looked up and from the corner of his eye he saw a figure dart out of sight behind the rock that topped the outcrop overlooking the wadi bed on the side farthest from where he had parked. He realized he had been watched from the moment the Land-Rover had bumped over the pebbled watercourse. He felt vulnerable yet at the same time had an urgent necessity to see the person who had been watching him. He opened the car door and slammed it, at the same time glancing upwards towards where the figure had disappeared. Immediately a head came into view: it was that of a young girl, her hair tied in a dark kerchief. For several seconds he stared at her, then his face relaxed into a smile. The girl continued to stare back at him, her expression of uncertainty unchanged, then she rose to her feet so that she was standing above him, her hands at her side. She was dressed in a loose black garment that came down almost to her bare feet. He smiled again, this time more to himself as he brought to mind her having been watching him.

He put his hand back on the door handle, let it rest there too long and felt it burning his palm. He withdrew it sharply and was about to wrap it round with the end of his shirt when, without warning, she raised her hand and a stone circled above him and landed beyond the oleanders. A billy goat blundered through the heap of tin cans and joined the rest of the flock. Taking off his sunglasses, he was momentarily blinded by the naked light.

Dangling the glasses in his left hand, he raised his other arm in a gesture that recognized her presence.

'*Bint!*' he called as he felt urged to say something. Then, on the spur of the moment, he added the one word, '*Moy,*' and leaned his head back and pointed his thumb at his mouth with fist closed, indicating that he wanted to drink. The thought crossed his mind that, even if she had any water, it wouldn't be safe to drink.

She held his gaze but did not react to his request. He changed his glasses to his right hand and put his other under his shirt and quickly opened the car door. Suddenly, in a shrill voice that startled him, she called scoldingly to her goats and hurled another stone to the far side of the water–course. The action brought sharp explosive gruntings from the goats as they scattered then formed up again in a group farther up the wadi bed. He looked at her again but she no longer seemed to be aware of his presence. He had only to seat himself behind the driving-wheel and he would be on his way to Dubai with no more to tell of the encounter than that he had seen a Bedouin girl with her goats. Once again, without reason, he invoked that word, one of the dozen or so that he knew, as though it were some charm that demanded to be spoken: '*Moy?*' he asked.

He felt slightly breathless as he awaited her reply, as though his life hung in its balance. This time she shook her head and looked away. Behind her the mountain range circled round but gave no sign of a habitation or of palm trees or vegetation. Perhaps she had come from some Bedouin encampment. He put the glasses back on and held out the freed hand and moved the four fingers towards himself, summoning her with a gesture he had seen Arabs use. She answered with a petulant toss of the head so that he saw her face in profile, the neck and ear bare of any ornament.

He stepped forward and became aware of the tightness of his shorts round his loins. He moved across the pebbles towards the steep pathway that led to the ledge on which she stood. She uttered two or three words to him which he didn't understand. He continued the climb, so steep at times that he was bent nearly double, scrabbling with both hands at stones and clumps of coarse grass. Again he became aware of the sun striking at the back of his neck; again the girl shouted something, this time in a voice strident with alarm.

Panting with the exertion, he arrived at the ledge. He looked about him and saw that the small plateau had been smoothed out. The sand bore marks of bare feet, and in the shade of the dominant rock lay a leather pouch with a shoulder strap and a goatskin tied at the neck with twine; a small pile of loose stones had been arranged alongside these objects. From this vantage point he could see a dark stain interrupting the brown range of mountains: a cluster of dirt-coloured huts at a distance of some two or three miles, separated by the greenness of date-palms. She was nowhere to be seen and the thought came to him that she might have hidden on the other side of the rock. He then became aware of her standing halfway up the path he had just climbed. She must have slipped round behind the rock and slithered down the slope to where she now stood. As their eyes met, her face puckered into a frown. He pointed to the ground where the goatskin lay and she answered with words he didn't understand.

Performing actions as though part of a ritual, he stooped down and took hold of the goatskin, then beckoned to her. He was angered when she appeared to take no notice of him. Didn't she understand he meant her no harm?

Her eyes met his in a gaze of hostility before she turned her back on him and walked into the wadi bed. Hearing him follow her, she glanced over her shoulder and he saw fear in the twist of her mouth. Running, he caught up with her as she reached the patch of sand in which the oleanders grew. As her hands clawed at his arms encircling her waist, the hope died within him that there would be any understanding between them. She struggled and he turned her round so that she faced him and he pressed her tightly against himself. He felt that if only she would stop fighting him, he would be content just to stand there with the hardness of his body touching hers. He saw small beads of sweat on her forehead and on the sparse hairs on her upper lip. He brought his hand up to her head, tore off the kerchief and grasped her hair. He lowered his lips to her mouth but she closed her lips tightly and moved her head from side to side, hoarsely muttering some words. A renewed spell of anger rose up in him at his inability to communicate with her. He forced her on to her knees, then on to her back. For a while he lay inertly over her as though this were all he sought of her. Then, with a renewal of energy, he wedged his knee between her thighs. He crouched above her, one hand holding her down, while with the other he dragged down his shorts, then ripped open her undergarment. He looked down at her sparse pubic hair, hardly visible against the dark skin, and the childish fold of her sex that had nothing in common with the pictures of coy, pouting women with trimmed triangles of hair that were torn out of girlie magazines and adorned the walls of the Staff House. He withdrew his hand from her lower face and tried to will her to look at his swollen sex: even such a concession on her part might somehow break the spell. She lay still for a while, breathing heavily with the efforts she had made against him, her eyes closed against the sun. Then her body stiffened and he saw that her eyes were wide open and were fixed in a stare at the ledge on which she had been standing. A hollowness of dread burrowed deep inside him.

Glancing over his shoulder, he saw no one and in the same instant knew that there had been no one there.

With horror he felt a loosening of his lower body. He fell back on his heels and in a desperate movement clasped hold of himself, as though seeking to stem the life-blood flow from a severed artery. Convulsive movements, remote and pleasureless, as uncontrollable as the voiding of vomit, pumped the semen between his fingers.

He made no attempt to stop the girl from scrambling to her feet. For a while he was aware of her standing some paces from him, conscious that she was no longer in any danger.

With the strength of the sun's rays striking against the back of his neck, he walked the few paces to the Land-Rover. Something glinted among the stones and he saw his sunglasses, the frames twisted and one of the lenses splintered, lying among goat droppings. He knew he should pick them up but lacked the strength of mind and body. As he climbed into the cabin he heard the snorting of the goats against the deep silence.

He turned the ignition key, put the engine into gear and, with both hands gripping the steering-wheel, moved forward across the pebbled wadi bed. The cabin was stale with the stench of his futile orgasm. He knew that he should return and retrieve the broken glasses which could prove his undoing. A ball of fear collected inside his chest and tears smarted at the back of his eyes. Behind him he heard the rattle of stones striking against the rear of the Land-Rover.

15
Two Worlds

His mother's sing-song voice carried shrilly from the veranda to the servants' quarters, calling his name. Peter kept quiet and gave a sideways glance at the group of Africans squatting in front of him — a white boy in khaki shorts and safari jacket and with sandals on his bare feet. He grimaced and raised a conspiratorial finger to his lips, then grinned at his friends. He knew that his mother would sometimes call two or three times and then give up, thinking that maybe he'd gone off somewhere with his servant Shereef. He reckoned he could stay on another ten or fifteen minutes before having to return to the house. This time, though, when the call was repeated, there was something insistent about the tone. He looked at

Shereef and drew down his mouth in an expression of exasperation. He signalled to Zidolo, the head boy, for him to pass him the cigarette for a final drag. He cupped his hand round the cigarette and sucked in the smoke through the small gap between his first finger and thumb. This was the way he had been taught to smoke a shared cigarette so that your lips didn't touch it. He felt a slight dizziness at the extra effort required to draw in the smoke; he then held it for a while in his mouth before blowing it out in a great cloud. He knew from experience that if he tried to swallow the smoke as they did he would feel even worse. Once he'd almost disgraced himself by being sick.

He passed the cigarette back to Zidolo, rose to his feet and walked slowly between the several dusty mango trees towards the whitewashed house with the mosquito-netted veranda that skirted it on three sides. He hoped that his mother would see that he was obeying her and would not call out yet again. Her high-pitched voice when summoning him back to the house was a subject of joking between himself and the servants. Now, at his back, he could imagine Mwanzi, the oversized cook, mouthing a soundless imitation of her. But though she had certainly seen his figure approaching through the trees, she nevertheless called out again: 'Peet ... er. Peet ... er.'

'Mummy, I'm coming,' he growled. 'I'm not deaf, you know.'

'And don't talk to your mother in that tone of voice,' replied his mother as he went slowly up the steps and joined her on the veranda. A tall, thin woman with muscular arms, she waited for him to raise his head to her before saying: 'And why are you always sitting down there with the servants? I hope they've not been feeding you any of their strange foods.'

'No,' he answered from under scowling brows, then wondered whether she would be able to smell the smoke on his breath.

'Go and have your bath,' she said to him,' and then you can have your supper. We're having people in to bridge and dinner tonight.'

'Can I play some hands?' he asked eagerly.

'If you're good,' she said and ruffled his hair, a gesture that always annoyed him.

'Who are they?' he asked.

'Dr and Mrs Simpson.'

'Oh,' he said in what he thought was an offhand tone.

'She's nice, isn't she?' his mother said archly.

'Yes,' he acknowledged and tried to stop himself from blushing. It was Julie Simpson who had taught him to do the crawl at the club swimming pool. Since then he found himself often thinking of her in her white swimsuit with her full bronzed legs and arms and her breasts which showed white when she leaned forward.

His mother again ruffled his hair. 'Off you go

then,' she told him, turning him round in the direction of the side door.

He enjoyed it when his parents had people in to dinner and bridge. There were always some titbits — or 'toasties' as they were known — which they had with their whiskies and soda and which he would be invited to hand round. He would be asked to help himself to one, and he generally succeeded in having four or five in the evening. Bridge would be played both before and after dinner, and in the before-dinner session his mother often let him play some of her hands. Otherwise he got no practice with his bridge as his father refused to make up the third in the three-handed version in which each player bid for dummy. 'It's not bridge,' he complained, '— more like poker if you ask me.'

While soaking in the bath, wondering whether his mother would come in and insist on scrubbing his back, he heard the sound of a car coming up the drive, then Dr Simpson's voice bellowing out some words. 'And how's the son and heir?' he heard Dr Simpson enquire, as he and his wife came up the front steps.

Peter's father made a jocular reply and everyone laughed.

'Hopefully he's in a bath scraping some of the mud off his knees,' his mother told them and again there was laughter.

Peter gave a cursory look at his knees and jumped out of the bath. He dried himself hurriedly and put on his pyjamas and dressing-gown which his mother had placed on a chair in the bathroom.

In the dining-room Zidolo was laying out the cutlery. Alongside the main dining-table a small one had been prepared for Peter's supper. He sat himself down and he and Zidolo exchanged glances with Peter bringing up his two hands to his mouth in the gesture of smoking a cigarette. Zidolo stifled a giggle as they heard his mother's quick footsteps approaching.

'You're having just the same as us,' his mother informed him: 'tomato soup to begin with, then your favourite fried fish and anchovy sauce. For pudding, instead of the Welsh rarebit we'll be having, I've opened you a tin of pears as a special treat.'

'Yummy!' said Peter.

What she omitted to tell him was that the grown-ups were also having a meat course: guinea-fowl and tinned asparagus.

While he was spooning up the soup, Peter could hear scraps of the conversation from the adjoining room where they had settled down to drinks and would soon be moving across to the bridge table with its baize top. Peter signalled to Zidolo to hurry in with his fish.

'She's got to the semi-finals,' he heard Dr Simpson say. 'Isn't that great?'

'Clever girl!' said Peter's mother. 'I don't see why you shouldn't win.'

'Oh, Pam's got a killing serve – more like a man's,' protested Julie Simpson. 'You know, she actually made the semi-finals a few years back in Nairobi. I'd be lucky to get a game off her. Anyway, I've got to beat Sally Onslow before that...'

Dr Simpson made a remark in a low voice and they all laughed.

'Don't forget about pitchers...' said Peter's mother in a jokey voice. 'But Sally as we all know has more things on her mind these days than tennis.'

'I suppose she had it coming,' said Peter's father.

'It's as much his fault as hers,' interposed Julie Simpson, and they carried on the conversation in hushed tones.

Peter cut up the slices of pear with his spoon and they slid tastelessly down his throat. He asked himself whether he really liked them as much as he claimed and wondered how he could manage to avoid having them again as a treat. He then heard the sound of the scraping of chairs as they moved to the bridge table.

'Cut for seats,' he heard his mother's voice.

'It's my say and I'm staying where I am,' pronounced Dr Simpson, slapping his two hands palms down on the table in front of him

'Cut for cards,' said his mother.

'Another king!' exclaimed Julie Simpson.

'I'll have the cards we cut with,' said Peter's father. There was a period of silence and Peter could imagine his father's rather ponderous way of dealing. Having dealt, he would tap his cards into a neat pile before picking them up and sorting them into suits.

Peter pushed back his chair silently, gave Zidolo a conspiratorial smile and walked through into the lounge. He waited till they became aware he was there, then said good-evening and walked towards his mother's chair.

'Evening, Peter,' said Julie Simpson, twisting round so that she faced him. 'Now come and say hallo properly.'

He felt himself redden as he walked over to her and her lips pursed against his cheek.

'Oh dear!' she exclaimed. 'Hey, come back, Peter – you mustn't compromise me by going about with lipstick on you.' She took her handkerchief and brought it up to her mouth and rubbed at his cheek. 'Now that's better,' she said.

Dr Simpson had led the laughter and Peter had tried to join in, though at the same time telling himself what a hateful person the doctor was. How could she have married such a man? She was obviously years younger. It seemed to him, too, from something he overheard when his parents were talking about 'Julie and the doctor', that she had been married before. This made her even more interesting.

He raised his eyes and found that Julie Simpson was looking at him and smiling, as though reading his thoughts. 'Heavens,' he told himself, 'she knows what I feel about her...' and he helped himself hurriedly to one of the halves of eggs that Zidolo had just come in with.

'P...p...' said his mother.

'Please,' he said automatically.

'Where were we?' interrupted his father, his mouth creased in irritation at the slow manner in which the game was proceeding. 'I said a heart, Julie said two clubs, and my partner raised me to two hearts.'

'No bid,' said Dr Simpson in the voice of someone who wished he had been dealt a better hand.

'Four hearts,' said Peter's father.

'I'm very tempted to double you but I won't,' said Julie Simpson, and she helped herself to one of the stuffed halves of eggs and congratulated Peter's mother on her cook.

'I was expecting something a bit better than that,' remarked Peter's father as his wife put down her hand as dummy. She was used to his making such comments so as to pave the way for his failing to make the contract. In fact, he went two down and remarked that his wife had badly overcalled her hand.

'Yes, he's a real treasure,' Peter's mother replied to Julie's remark, ignoring her husband's criticism of her call. 'He's fine just so long as he keeps off the booze.'

'They all drink given half a chance,' pronounced Dr Simpson.

'If they can get it,' remarked Julie Simpson.

'Oh, they make their own stuff. This *changa* of theirs is a lot more lethal than anything we've got,' commented Peter's father.

'Lethal's the word,' said Dr Simpson. 'That *changa* stuff can kill you' – and he launched into a long story about a patient of his who had a garden boy who went blind from drinking it.

'Whoever's dummy can fill up our glasses,' said Peter's mother, noticing that the large whisky she had given Dr Simpson was now no more than an ice-cube.

Peter, following the conversation, wondered whether he should contribute to it. He sensed that there would be dangers if he allowed himself to utter the sentence he had in readiness; he knew, too, that it would be merely showing off and could lead to questioning and perhaps to trouble for himself and his friends.

'Then there was the case of that gang of men up near Tororo who were making the stuff. It seems a couple of people died and the men were had up for murder,' Peter's mother recounted to them.

'That's right,' said Dr Simpson. 'It might be a lesson for other *changa*-makers if they hanged a couple of them.'

'The trouble is these people have been making the stuff since the dawn of history,' added Peter's father.

'Zidolo drinks only Dimple,' Peter suddenly found himself throwing down the statement like a challenging glove.

Silence descended on the four bridge players.

'What are you talking about, Peter?' demanded his father gruffly. He had been dealt a good hand and wanted to get on with the game.

'Yes,' said his mother, 'whatever are you trying to say?'

The thing he had both wanted and dreaded had occurred – he had become the centre of attention. He glanced towards Julie Simpson and saw her looking at him over her cards.

'Oh nothing,' he said, walking round to behind his mother's chair and taking a cheese straw on the way. 'They were just having a joke.'

'Come on, Peter,' said his father, 'we're all waiting for you to tell us what your friends at the bottom of the garden are up to.'

'Well...' said Peter, moving awkwardly to behind Julie Simpson's chair and wishing they would pick up their cards and go on with the game.

'Well?' insisted his mother.

'They were all drinking from one of those funny Dimple bottles.'

At that moment Zidolo made his entrance and everyone fell silent.

'Tell cook food twenty minutes,' Peter's mother told the head boy.

Once Zidolo had gone, Dr Simpson remarked: 'So they were quaffing Dimple Haig were they, my lad? Very nice too!'

Peter saw his father tap his cards impatiently on the table and suggest they get on with the game, that they only just had time to finish the rubber before dinner.

'Mummy, you promised me I'd play a hand,' said Peter, wiggling his body against his mother's chair.

'Don't whine like that,' his father said. He had been irritated by his son's revelation about the Dimple bottle but had no wish to discuss the matter in front of guests.

Peter continued to stand behind his mother's chair. Then, all at once, Julie Simpson laid her cards fanwise on the table with the words 'I'll give you just the two club tricks', and they all wrote down on their score-pads: four spades at 120 plus 30 for the overtrick and five hundred for rubber. Peter saw his father's glowering expression; apart from anything else, he didn't like losing.

'Now off you go, darling,' his mother said to him.

'But I didn't even play one hand,' he protested.

'There just wasn't time – we're all going into dinner now. Say good-night, there's a good boy.'

'Good-night,' he said and everyone said good-night back.

'You may take another cheese straw with you,' his mother told him.

'Take two,' Julie said with a wink. He smiled at her and took two, then again said good-night and left the room.

'I'll come and tuck you up when you're safely in bed,' his mother called after him. 'And don't forget to brush your teeth when you've finished those cheese straws.'

His mother, when she came to kiss him good-night, said nothing except, 'Now go to sleep and we'll have a talk in the morning.'

He fell asleep crying. He was ashamed, especially for having shown off like that in front of Julie Simpson. He was also frightened of having to face his father the next day. He realized that it would have been better had he been questioned then and there about the Dimple bottle when he would have been able to explain that the servants were behaving like children playing a game of pretence. After all, nothing had happened except that the night before he had seen Zidolo and the others drinking out of a Dimple Haig bottle. Only his own servant Shereef, the sole Muslim among them, had not taken part and had sat watching them with a mixture of amusement and contempt. They had passed the bottle back and forth, wiping the top with the palms of their hands. They had even offered the bottle to Peter, with wide grins on all their faces, but he had shaken his head and made a wry face to indicate that he wouldn't like the taste. He had wondered at the time how they had acquired it. When, later, he and

Shereef had got up to go and feed the birds he had caught and caged that afternoon, Shereef had told him that the others had put some of their own local brew into the bottle, an empty one thrown in the dustbin by Peter's mother several months ago.

Before going to sleep he assured himself that everything would turn out all right — he would simply add the information about the bottle containing some sort of local drink.

Peter found the following morning that his little joke had gained in seriousness, with his father having postponed going to the office in order to question him about it. He had given a scornful laugh when Peter told him that the Dimple bottle had contained nothing but local beer or some other native drink. How did he know? Had he tried it? For an instant Peter thought of saying that he had but feared that he might be getting into deeper trouble. The servants, his father pointed out, weren't children to play at games.

'They were just pretending, daddy.'

Peter stared into his father's stern face, the lips stretched thinly below the brushlike moustache. Why, suddenly, were the servants described as not being like children?

His mother entered the room and his father indicated by an upward turn of the eyes that their son had nothing further to say. As if Peter were not there, his parents asked one another how it was that the servants had managed to acquire the Dimple

Haig bottle. Hadn't his mother noticed that one was missing from the pantry store? Surely Zidolo couldn't have filched a bottle from the drinks' tray?

'Of course one of them could have collected an empty bottle from the garbage,' Peter's mother pointed out.

'That's what they did,' Peter said in a shrill voice. 'They were just pretending, daddy.'

'You'll make me really angry if you go on saying that to me' – and Peter could see that his father was in a blazing rage and had made up his mind. 'Why, if you thought they were playing some sort of stupid game, did you mention it at all? Just to try to get them into trouble?'

More than anything else this last suggestion probed deep into the area of his sense of guilt. His tears, kept at bay all this time, now choked him and his mother took him away to the bathroom and bathed his eyes and told him he had done right to report what he had seen. He pleaded with her not to do anything against Zidolo and the others but she told him that that was for his father to decide.

Before his father left for the office the decision. had been taken that the servants would be punished by having a week's pay deducted from their wages at the end of the month – all except for Shereef.

Peter was told of the decision. The servants would be paraded before his father at lunchtime when he came back from the office. Once again Peter tried pleading with his mother on behalf of the servants. He told her that they wouldn't be so stupid as to be drinking whisky they'd stolen from the house in front of him; they would know he would tell his parents.

'I don't think they would, my darling boy. I believe they all think of you as one of them. I've told you time and time again that you shouldn't sit around with them half the day as you do. You see the sort of trouble it causes everyone. You've got to learn that they live in a different world from ours.'

Taking his catapult, he went out with Shereef in search of pigeons in the neighbouring *shambas*. He told Shereef that his mother had discovered that there was a bottle of whisky missing from the storeroom. How else could he explain the train of events? Shereef insisted it had been an empty bottle that had been discarded, which had then been rescued and filled up with local beer. Peter asked him to warn the others of what had happened and that they would be questioned about it when the *bwana* returned from office.

The servants were called to line up on the front veranda. Peter's father had a cane chair brought out for him from which he addressed the six men standing in order of seniority. He told them briefly that his son had seen them drinking from a bottle of whisky. Where could that bottle of whisky have come from if not from the house in which they worked and from which they drew their wages? The men looked down at their feet saying nothing, then sideways at Zidolo, who in little more than a whisper told of how he had found the bottle several months back in the rubbish and had washed it out so that they could fill it with local beer.

'I don't believe you,' said Peter's father brusquely and he fined them each a week's wages, to be deducted at the end of the month. 'You're lucky I didn't bring the police into all this,' he ended up in a threatening tone. None of the servants uttered a word in protest.

When Peter's mother informed him what had been decided Peter protested: 'That's unfair. Why shouldn't daddy believe they found an empty bottle? He just fines them like that, knowing very well they can't do anything back.' He looked up into her face defiantly. 'They're my friends,' he told her, 'and daddy's being unfair.'

'And don't talk like that about your father,' she said, seizing him by the shoulder and shaking him. 'I've got a good mind to tell him what you said.'

'Tell him!' Peter retorted and ran off to his room.

He felt it no longer mattered what he did or said – there was nothing more he could lose. His friends would know that he had betrayed their trust and their response would be not to allow him ever again into their confidence: a door had been closed into a world that had been opened uniquely to him alone. From now on he would be barred from it and forced to make do with that other world inhabited by his parents and their friends.